WEB OF THE WORLDS

By
HARRY HARRISON and KATHERINE MacLEAN

I0616855

ARMCHAIR FICTION
PO Box 4369, Medford, Oregon 97501-0168

*For more information about Armchair Books and products, visit our
website at…*

www.armchairfiction.com

Or email us at…

armchairfiction@yahoo.com

SWEPT INTO AN ALTERNATE UNIVERSE...

He had always been something of a pampered individual, mild-mannered and physically daunted—his over-zealous mother had seen to that. However, that was before the Unicorn Ring lifted Grant O'Reilly's life strand and shoved it down among the ghouls, Berl-Cats, space aliens, and other unearthly creatures that he soon found himself surrounded by.

Now his utmost challenge was adopting to the new worlds he had been unwillingly thrust into. He must quickly develop the skills of a seasoned barbarian warrior or it would cost him his life. And it was only an untapped inner strength that could lead him back to the world he knew.

FOR A COMPLETE SECOND NOVEL, TURN TO PAGE 107

CAST OF CHARACTERS

GRANT O'REILLY
One minute he was getting married, the next minute he found himself on a frozen world with a mob screaming for his blood.

AKER AMEN
He was the quintessential warrior, from a world far beyond the realms of Earth—and O'Reilly owed him his life many times over.

TAFTHA LONG
She was a beautiful woman soldier that Grant was smitten with. Unfortunately she lived in a world besieged by aliens from space.

GRAYF
He was Amen's companion, just as rugged and just as fierce, but he decided to run when he should have stood and fought.

THE GOOD DUKE DARIKUS
His vast army was waiting to attack. Unfortunately his plans were held up by poor dice rolls and a bad case of gout.

THE HOLY MEN OF AL'KAHAR
They looked like zombies in black robes, but they were fierce warriors who would kill you and eat your rotting remains!

FOREWARD

The Three Norns, weavers of men's destiny, sit in the dusty hall of eternity with the glittering tapestry of the dimensions before them. Their aged fingers move tirelessly over the strands—twisting, weaving and joining in an infinity of combinations.

Each strand is a life. As they guide the strands they guide the lives. Their voices rise and fall in a constant murmur; they pass the single eye, one to the other, to watch the weaving of this incredible fabric. The voices grow louder, their tones change. Man's destiny is not always smooth.

"No, stop, you cannot bring that world line here."

"It makes the pattern."

"It makes the pattern worse. I will have to make changes in my section."

"Destroyed, I say; ruined. The work of centuries!"

The voices grow louder, there is a hint of anger in the tones. "Stop, Grissel, stop. Those changes cannot be made." Her hand flicks across the tapestry in an angry gesture.

There is a ring on the middle finger, the Unicorn Ring. The ring brushes the surface and the Unicorn's horn catches in one of the tiny glittering threads of a human life—and pulls it loose.

"I'll do it my way—give me the eye."

The argument continues. The thread of a man's fate floats unattached in space, unnoticed.

CHAPTER ONE

"Sorry, mother, it doesn't fit."

"I got it in your size, Granty," Grant's mother said firmly. "Try it on again and see if it really doesn't fit."

Grant O'Reilly tried it on. He knew very well that it wouldn't fit, and it didn't. The coat was tight across the shoulders and his wrists stuck three inches of cuff out past the sleeves. He had gotten used to this kind of thing. His mother had bought all his clothes for the wedding, and as usual she had assumed he was younger than he was and gotten everything too small. This time it was serious. It was Sunday, and they had come a long way out of town for his wedding in this small church where Lucy's aunts and uncles and cousins had been married. There was no chance of buying or renting a morning coat.

He looked at himself in the mirror, trying to see himself in the eyes of Lucy's poised and influential relatives. No, it wouldn't do. Lucy would be dismayed, ashamed of him with his wrists sticking out like a gawky farm boy. He tried to tug the sleeves down. Today of all days, he had to look sophisticated, the way Lucy liked him to be.

His reflection stared back calfishly from the pier glass and made the same plucking gestures at the jacket cuffs. He didn't really like this tall, thin young fellow with the ash-blond hair. The eyebrows were so light that they were almost invisible, giving the face a gentle, saintly expression. When he was away from mirrors he always imagined himself stronger and darker—the fit husband and defender of a lovely woman like Lucy.

Lucy! A warm glow flushed his face at the thought of her.

It was more of a physical thought than a spiritual one and he felt that it somehow didn't belong in church. He turned from the glass and tried to shrug off the jacket and the thought at the same time.

Herb Collomb slumped in his chair against the far wall and puffed composedly on his ancient pipe. The strength in his solid form gave Grant a feeling of security—the same way it had done all the way through college. They had roomed together and graduated together. It was only fitting that Herb be his best man. Herb grinned around his pipe and Grant was surprised to find himself grinning back.

The vestry window was open and a warm breath of spring air blew in. A bird was singing somewhere outside; the whole world seemed very wonderful to Grant.

Then he looked at the ill-fitting coat he held in his hand and felt the unhappy tension building up inside himself. How could he get a new coat? But it was already too late to do anything; he could hear the warming-up notes of the organ and the shuffling feet of the guests entering the chapel. He muttered a repressed damn.

"Don't swear, Grant. I'm sure Lucy would be very hurt if she heard you talk like that. She's from a very good family."

"I'm sorry, mother."

"That's right, dear. I always want to be proud my son is a gentleman."

Herb dropped his pipe and picked it up, looking somewhat red in the face.

Grant tried to smile, and then felt the old, sinking change coming. He tried to stop it. No, not now! Why did it have to be now? Once or twice in his life—by a great effort—he had managed to postpone an attack when its timing was bad.

But he would not be able to hold it back through the entire wedding. Better to get it over with and not spoil the wedding later. All he had to do was to get away from the voices and eyes and be alone for awhile. There was a thin ringing in his ears, coming closer. He stopped fighting it and let it come.

"There's ten minutes yet," he said, hastily over the singing in his ears and the feeling of growing distance between himself and all others. "I'm going to step out in the fresh air a moment."

There was a comfortable old graveyard outside, with slanted stones and long green grass and a gnarled peach tree in full bloom. It was cut off from the outside world and the passage of time by a high stone wall. The side door of the vestry opened to a little flagged path that curved around the building, away from the observing eyes of windows. A private place for a moment at least.

"I have to avoid excitement," Grant thought, letting the door shut behind him. It was too late to avoid it now; he'd have to take his medicine. Anyone watching would have seen Grant's lips curl back from his teeth in an unhappy grimace that showed irregular canine teeth and changed his angelic appearance to a rather pleasant animal look, like a blond bird dog. He wandered on, past thought with the pounding in his head, unconsciously seeking a sheltered spot to let go. He found it, a deep right angle in the stone wall where it turned. He blundered off the path and into it and leaned forward against the wall, propped himself in a corner and waited for the petite mal, the time of stone-like unconsciousness.

There was no knowing how much time had passed, but the sudden pressure was gone and the thin ringing in his ears, and he could see and hear and feel again. He leaned there a moment longer, grateful for the cool roughness of the stone against his forehead, thankful that he was not the kind who fell down and thrashed around. He could go stand quietly in the bathroom with the door shut and not frighten Lucy with it when they were married.

The sickness had deprived him of the games of childhood, hedged him around with the watchful care of his mother. It had taken away his freedom to risk and dare, leaving him only the second-hand adventures of poetry and books, but he was not going to let it take his marriage away from him. His hard-learned ability to feel the fit coming would let him live a normal life and earn money as an architect without his clients ever seeing anything wrong with him. With warning enough, there was always a quiet place where he could go to have an attack.

He turned and looked out across the greenness of the deep grass and the old stone wall with the small sandstone tombstones slanting right and left; everything was more vivid, as if sight were cleansed.

There was a window above his head and he could hear his mother's voice trickling out, very clear and distant, like a memory. "Granty has fits, you know. If he gets excited, that is. It took me a great deal of trouble to get him exempted from athletics at all his schools without saying what his trouble was. His father had fits, too; they began after we were married. Such a sweet man. It runs in the family. They're sensitive, you know."

He ignored the unhappy feeling the words gave him and told himself that everything she did was for his good. She would take care of the jacket, too; she always fixed things so they came out the right way. He stood up to return inside.

Then he saw it.

It was long and white and huge. It was like a giant bar or an elephant's tusk stretching across the sky from horizon to horizon. One instant it was as far away as eternity; the next it was swooping down towards him. He couldn't tell where that awareness came from, but he knew it was true. It was coming directly towards him. It was like being on the tracks in front of an express train.

Before he could scream—before the thought that formed the scream was fully born—it was too late. It struck without impact—softly with a sudden sensation of tremendous motion.

The world vanished. In his eye he could see the after-image of the graveyard, the orange of the grass and the red of the sky. The bright colors slowly faded and were replaced by nothing.

That was the only word that described the sensations he felt. At first his mind went out in an expanding spiral of fear, then contracted back to something like sanity. He felt nothing; he heard nothing. What he saw was puzzling until he realized it was no-color. It was also not black. It was nearest to gray, a gray fog of velvet that pressed in on him from all sides.

With a heart-stopping shock he realized that he wasn't breathing. But his heart couldn't stop, because it wasn't beating. All the functions of his body were dead.

I am dead.

The thought had been scratching at the surface of his mind and now it gibbered its way in. His tightly held thoughts collapsed and his mind screamed out in madness.

There was no measurement of time or duration, so Grant had no idea how long the period lasted. It could have been years or seconds, but slowly it ebbed away. After the insanity came thoughts, but they helped no more than the madness; he had no idea where he was nor what had happened. After the thoughts came boredom, and this lasted for eternity.

His mind became like his body and he hung there in the unchanging gray fog, changeless himself, and waited.

CHAPTER TWO

"Look now! Look what you've done. You've pulled one of the threads loose."

"I never—you're the one who did it when you were screaming at me that the pattern was wrong."

"Well the pattern is wrong…"

The argument continued and the second sister leaned forward to shout her opinion. The loose thread blew in her face and in anger she shoved it back into the fabric.

She did not weave it back into the pattern but pushed it in at random and returned to the argument.

Abruptly the grayness and silence was smashed by a screaming clamor and Grant found himself falling through air that seemed thick with sound. A filthy board floor came up and smote him, and he lay stunned for a moment amid the clamor of drunken howls, the smash of breaking bottles, the leathery thud and grunt of blows meeting flesh. Yellow light flickered in his eyes and shadows surged above him, snarling.

There was a crunching thud almost directly above him and a man with a short scraggly beard and overlong hair tumbled heavily across Grant's legs. Blood began oozing from his ragged hair, and the shape of his head looked horribly dented.

With a reflex of revulsion, Grant yanked free from beneath the limp hulk and rose to a half crouch. A man had just been killed and dropped on top of him, and no one paid any attention. The crowd and howls had surged a way from him and were somewhere else now, although running forms still went past to plunge into it.

Smoke of flickering tapers, the fumes of cooking, the stench of spilled wine and aged food assailed his nostrils and stung his eyes, but he could make out that the room was as big as a barn, with hand-hewn beams close overhead, reflecting back noise and heat and light, and further up, a roof lost in smoky shadows. The beams seemed to waver in the flickering light with the fury of the human sounds coming from below them.

The screaming crowd had grown until it was close again, but their backs were toward him. Ragged hair hung down below their ears; they waved staffs, daggers, and broken bottles threateningly, shouting at someone in the middle. Filthy shirts of rough brown, like burlap, covered each back, hanging over dirty fur pants.

Grant straightened and found that he was tall enough to see over the heads to the maelstrom in the center of the mob.

The crowd was attacking a big man who had his back to one of the supporting pillars. As Grant watched, the man lunged with a grunting shout, swung a sweeping blow with a long sword, flung himself back, fended a descending pole from his head with the flat of the sword, smashed back another with a thing like an iron Indian club in his left hand, carried the smash through with a lunge to the head of the staff wielder with a crunch, and lunged back to the pillar again. He moved in jerky stops and starts and retreats of extraordinary energy, slashing, and fending, grunting in a half shout with each effort.

The athleticism of it was astonishing, but that wasn't what froze Grant. It was the man's costume. The dull brown shine of leather armor, like a picture in an encyclopedia, the glint of chain mail, the broadsword, and the Indian club thing—a mace? It was something out of pre-medieval history. What was he doing here? For a moment, his eyes searched for a camera. But this was real blood, not ketchup.

Where was the way out? Crouching with the wary immobility of a hunted animal, Grant turned his head. Thick benches and tables were scattered around the empty half of the room, tapers flickered in bowls and added smoke to the murky air, overturned tables and spilled bottles littered the floor. Where was the door? The dimness and smoke confused his eyes, the ghastly sounds rocked in his brain. Where in the name of sanity were there even windows? What kind of place was this?

He moved away from the mob sounds, putting a long table between himself and the battle, but a crescendo howl turned him in time to see the end. The fighter in leather armor was temporarily confused; his sword lodged in a pole where its edge had turned and cut into the wood. He stood trying to free his sword. A pole, jabbed like a spear, took him in the cheekbone with a blow that canted his head over. His sword pulled free as he was hit, but he had no time to lift it. Jolted back and forth under the thud of heavy staffs finding him at last, hit savagely on all sides at once, the thickset man in barbarian armor staggered a few steps further from the protecting pillar. With a joint-less look of unconsciousness and broken bones he pitched headlong in Grant's direction.

Grant broke out of his frozen trance and began to back off, still staring, feeling his way by grip on the splintery boards of the table behind him. Staffs rose and fell over the thing on the floor and daggers flashed, and he was thankful that the triumphant howling drowned out some of its sound. This might be a nightmare, but death in this nightmare was as real as any butchery.

The howl died and men mumbling and cursing and nursing bruises and wounds began to look around. Grant still sidled slowly backward, depending on their attention being held by the dead thing on the floor, while one of the triumphant attackers bent over it, and pried loose the sword from a dead hand. As he raised it toward the ceiling in a triumphant drunken arc, his eyes found Grant and saw him moving. Being seen by one of these creatures of a nightmare was carrying nightmare too far. Grant froze between the instinct to turn and run and the hope of being ignored.

A snaggle-toothed grin split the face of the man who had seen him. *"Kill the blasphemer!"* He put a foot on a bench and leaning over the table separating them and swung at Grant with a clumsy two-handed blow. *"Blood for N'tigh'ta!"*

Grant moved sidewise because he could not go back. The sword sank three inches into the next table behind him, revealing at this close inspection a huge bloody length and a heaviness that was more like an extended axe blade, a terrible weapon that could split a man in half. As the other struggled to free it, Grant leaped around the end of the table and ran, feeling as if he moved on leaden legs. Shouts and howls sounded behind him. He ran toward one end of the room where it was darker. A human figure was dimly visible, and something beyond him that might be a door. A few more strides and, straining his eyes, Grant saw a wide, closed door. He could also see that the man who stood in front of it was raising an ax, waiting for him, grinning.

Grant stopped. He stopped the easy way, by running into a table. There were howls behind him, coming closer, but near him was a ladder, leaning against one of the foot-square rafters that held up the roof. It took half a second to reach it. He pulled himself weakly up the rungs and onto a transverse beam, then turned and kicked the ladder into the faces of the screaming mob below.

For a moment he felt safe. There weren't as many down there as he had thought; the main crowd seemed to be howling elsewhere in the building after another victim. Nevertheless, four men below him still seemed interested in him. They glared up with their ragged hair in their eyes, and shouted curses about the stain that had to be washed from N'tigh'ta, whatever that was. Those who had staves struck at his legs. Their aim was drunken and missed him, but the grinning lout with the sword was heaving its monstrous length into the air again, and another one had picked up a stool. A staff struck Grant a painful blow on the ankle and he saw he could not stay where he was. He did something he would never have had courage to do an hour earlier. He released his clutch on the vertical pillar and turned and ran along the beam he stood on. It was less than a foot wide and uneven. Under other circumstances he would have fallen off, but to fall now meant death, so he managed to stay on, although every successful step was a constant astonishment to him. Half running, Grant staggered the last ten feet and collapsed panting against a central pillar. From this vantagepoint he had a wide view of the barn-like place.

A small group of the fur-pants were struggling with the ladder that he had kicked down, attempting to right it and follow him. Three blowsy-looking women and a fat man were huddling in a gigantic fireplace against the far wall. But below Grant's feet was the center of the noise.

The whole howling mob that had downed the other soldier, and twice as many besides, seemed to be pressing in around another swordsman with his back toward the pillar Grant was clutching. Massive shoulders and thick arms encased in seemingly inadequate coverings of scarred red leather armor swung in and out with a long sword that seemed from Grant's vantage to be even more huge than the terrible weapon that had missed him a few moments earlier. A heavy barbed mace in the big swordsman's left hand made abrupt occasional swings that contacted encroaching staves, daggers, or arms with an equal sounding thud and smash, leaving nothing that it touched unbroken.

The athletic energy of the other big soldier had been phenomenal, but as Grant looked down on the glittering, weaving sweep of sword he saw a skill that smoothed away effort and wove a web of steel around the swordsman. The man combined parries and slashes into one unfaltering swing that curved back along its deadly course without ever stopping or slowing when it sliced through wood and flesh and bone, its deadly force not in any separate surge of the arm that swung it, but in the whispering speed of the heavy blade. It was as smooth and dangerous as the singing circle of a propeller, and the mob feared it.

Snarling with drunken fury, they still stayed back from the circle and tried blows at long range, or threw daggers and knives that rang against metal and were smashed aside before reaching the soldier.

Not all of them had been cautious; red-throated and split-skulled corpses lay within the circle and men dragged themselves apart from the crowd, groaning and nursing broken arms. One was being helped by another to wrap up a bleeding, handless stump.

The soldier sang and shouted as he swung his sword, a wordless chant that fitted the dance of its glittering edge. As Grant watched, he stepped out, grunted with an extra surge and swayed forward in a balanced half step that reached the blood-wet tip of the sword a foot further in its circuit and was rewarded by three separate shrieks from three directions. The encircling mob crowded back, cursing and striking each other in their haste, and resumed formation at a more respectful distance, leaving another of their number on the floor curled up around a half severed arm, trying to staunch the red life that pumped from it, dying and not worth the extra stroke that would kill him.

The big soldier was holding his own, but he could not hold that web work of steel and speed around him forever. He was panting in his chant. Already the crowd had circled behind the pillar. One slip, one falter, and a concerted rush from all sides would overwhelm him.

Grant found he regretted it. Such skill and delight as the big soldier showed in his bloody work was a kind of art and deserved life. Then he realized that when the soldier went, it would be his turn. It was only the singing circle of the soldier's blade that cleared space where the crowd could not swarm under his beam and batter him down. When the soldier died, Grant would go, too.

Grant clutched at the smoke-blackened wood as a surge of nausea tore at his bowels. What was he doing in this impossible place? Had he been struck by a car and was this all just a feverish dream?

As if to answer, a hurtling bottle crashed against his chest. The blow and the jagged tear in his vest were real, as well as the ache in his ankle where a staff had struck him. He reached a sick certainty that even if this were a dream, it would be safer to treat it as hard, merciless fact. There seemed to be a good chance that his death here would be as final as any he would ever have.

The ladder was finally propped against the further end of the beam and the men below were pushing and scrambling to see who would be first up it. Fur-pants with the sword climbed up three rungs, only to be hit in the back of the neck by fur-pants with the stool. As he dropped off, the one with the stool scrambled up, followed closely by the five or six others. Weaving, but keeping their feet easily, they ran along the beam toward Grant.

The one with the stool stopped at a good range and swung the stool back over his head for a skull-crushing blow. The ones behind were not ready for that sudden stop and pushed into him, pushing him closer, and at the same instant, Grant realized that he needed a weapon. Taking advantage of the stool-man's unbalance and hesitation, Grant leaned forward and gripped a leg of the stool and yanked. His yank had force because he kept a hold on the central pillar with his other arm, but fur-pants with the stool had a strong grip on the other legs, and was too befuddled to let go. He was yanked off his feet. With a hoarse shout of anger, the man dove down into the soldier's private battleground of clear floor below; badly entangled with the stool, he landed and had his throat neatly slit by a casual side sweep of the whispering sword.

The big soldier looked up, thinking he was being attacked from above. His face split in an immense grin as he saw Grant facing a line of attacking men.

"Oho! A friend." He paused, completing another swing around the circle below that was answered with one pained curse, and shifted his position a little, glancing back up at Grant. "And just in time, too!"

In the natural course of some pattern he was weaving, as though without his effort, the sword extended its range in a backhand curve and licked up over the edge of the beam, cutting the ankles from under the first two men; they tottered, ankle tendons severed, tripping on their limp dangling feet, and fell into the mob. The next man tried to retreat, but only succeeded in unbalancing the unsteady file behind him. As they began to topple off they added to the confusion below, and for a moment the mob drew back, thinking it was being attacked by enemies from above.

The soldier stuck his blood-encrusted mace into a loop on his belt while he drove the circle further back with savage advances and then made a rush to the pillar, as though to clear away the few lurking behind it. There was only one, who leaped backward and tumbled over a bench. In the shadow behind the pillar, where it would not be immediately clear to the mob what he was doing, the soldier laughed and stuck a free hand up to Grant.

"Come on, mate, give us a lift up and we'll soon be out of here."

It was the first friendly word Grant had heard among what had seemed a million howls of hate and murder, and suddenly everything seemed more sane and matter of fact, like the friendly commonsense tone of the soldier. Rapidly but without hysteria, Grant knelt on the beam, locked his right arm around the vertical pillar, and extended his left down to be grasped. He felt a callused hand grip his.

As the soldier pulled himself up, Grant thought his arm would be wrenched apart at every joint. He bit down on a scream of pain. Still gripping his sword, the big man hooked its hilt over the beam and pulled himself the rest of the way up. He came up smoothly, but most of his weight had been on Grant's arm, and the man was even bigger and thicker with muscle than he had looked from below. At least three hundred pounds of man and equipment had heaved himself up on the tensile strength of one thin, slightly undernourished arm.

Ignoring a clatter of bottles, daggers and small objects that sailed past, the soldier was sheathing his sword and peering into the darkness at the end of the room. He stepped onto the right-angle beam without a glance at Grant, and began to move toward the rear wall. Grant went after him, rubbing his aching arm, but oddly pleased because this time he walked on a narrow beam without a tremor.

As they walked, the roof slanted down closer until Grant could see a low clerestory with sealed windows facing them; above that the smoke-blackened roof angled up into the shadows. The soldier rapped the wall with his pommel and looked satisfied, as though he had found a way out.

Gesturing to Grant to crowd in close, the soldier pointed to the wall, which was hung with shapes like pairs of full sacks and things that looked like festoons of dried weeds.

There was a rancid food-like smell in the air and Grant realized that the noxious looking things were probably cured meat and herbs. The soldier unhooked two linked hams and draped them over Grant's shoulders. They were massive, pulling him down with a staggering weight for which he was unprepared, seeing them handled so lightly. Grant found himself over the edge and falling, and was brought back onto the beam by a lightning grip and heave of the soldier.

The man grunted a derogatory remark to himself, and then laughed, braced his hands against an overhead timber and began kicking boards out of the side of the building.

For a moment Grant doubted his eyes; the soldier was husky and big, but even a superman should not put holes in a building with a few kicks. Yet the soldier continued to kick, loosening and dispatching another board. Grant had learned about crooked contractors substituting flimsy workmanship in his studies of architecture. The *thunk* of the boards under the soldier's kicks was not the sound of seasoned timber. As the second kicked board leaned outward and vanished, Grant decided that the sidewalls had probably been fastened on with old chewing gum or something of equal strength, and dismissed the problem. A deeper darkness showed where the boards had been and icy air and snowflakes swirled in instead of the spring sunshine he had vaguely expected. The big man at the opening hardly hesitated for a deep breath before crouching at the edge and leaping out of sight.

Grant, balancing groggily on the beam, looked at the darkness outside. It was not inviting. His moment of indecision ended as a pole reached up and cracked his shin. To stay would be to condemn himself to a peculiarly undignified and butcherish kind of death at the hands of a particularly bestial mob. Other forms of death were to be preferred. He shuffled to the edge and tottered there.

Clutching his hams, he made a hampered attempt to crouch at the edge and leap outwards as the big swordsman had done. He tried and toppled through into frigid, snow filled darkness.

CHAPTER THREE

The snow outside had drifted and banked high against the building wall. Grant sank into it and floundered helplessly until his head came above the surface.

He could not remember ever having been so uncomfortable before. His body was bruised and sore, the hams hung like a dead weight around his neck, melted snow was soaking into his clothes, and the air, when he came up and encountered it, was icy and filled with flying particles that stung against his face.

His surroundings were completely invisible, a black wilderness of cold. A shout reached him from somewhere ahead and Grant floundered toward the sound to a place where the drifts were only waist high and the wind cut through his thin dress suit like an icy lash. A few yards further and he found what appeared to be a path where other bodies had floundered before him and lowered the snow a little. He jumped as a hand clutched him out of the darkness.

"Follow me, mate—and don't lose those hams or I'll tear out your skinny throat." The soldier moved off, ploughing a shallow channel in the deep snow, and Grant floundered after him.

His shoes were pointed, black, shiny and expensive—or had been when he had last seen them. He couldn't see them now, but he could feel them. They were fine for dancing or getting married in, but they were worse than useless for walking in the snow. Soaked and soggy, they squished with every step. Grant shoved through the clutching drifts and felt sorry for himself.

He had thought of asking the trudging form ahead to stop and let him rest, but he had the horrible thought miles back that if he stopped he would freeze to death. This was the only thing that enabled him to put one numbed foot in front of the other. He had followed the swordsman, expecting him momentarily to arrive at a house or some warm place; it would be impossible that the man was content to plough through endless hellish snow. But he had long ago given up thinking about when they would arrive at the warm place, or where they were going, and just stumbled after the moving man ahead, as if he were warmth itself, always retreating, always out of reach.

The darkness was passing and the sky was brightening—showing the wastes of snow around him. Even light seemed to hurt with the bitter numbness of nerves that were almost frozen.

In the growing light he saw small trees on either side. They thickened until the men were threading in and around large trees in a woods thick enough to stop the biting wind and allow only a thin layer of snow to cover its floor. Grant followed the man in barbarian armor over the clearer ground, his mind awakening and beginning to ask unanswerable questions, until they emerged from the trees into the cold and the drifting deep snow again.

Closing his eyes against the bite of wind, Grant tried to stop sensation and thought. They ploughed across a rutted path that might have been a road under the snow, and then down a slope with trees, the soldier going faster, and Grant keeping up because it was easier to stagger downhill. The wind got behind and hurried him, putting knives of cold into his back.

Down in a hollow ahead, sheltered from the wind, a small campfire flickered. Grant's first realization that they had reached their journey's end was when a hoarse voice called out...

"Hold there! Who is it?" There was the quick rasp of a sword being slipped from the scabbard.

"Aker Amen and some hams—make room by the fire, you lazy sons!"

The soldier pushed up to the blaze, with Grant tottering eagerly after him. Before he could reach its beckoning warmth, the man with the sword jumped forward and clutched him by the shirtfront.

"Aker, this isn't Bigeln! What happened to him—and who is this wreck with the meat necklace?"

Aker Amen toasted his wet feet and frowned into the fire. "Bigeln was a fool and now he's dead. I would be too, except that this stranger came along and we managed to get out of that filthy spowl's nest together. Let him be."

The swordsman let go of Grant's coat. Since this was the only thing holding him up, Grant collapsed in a limp heap. One of the hams plopped into the mud next to Aker Amen, who produced a dagger from his belt and calmly sawed himself off a piece of meat. He chewed the tough flesh and ruminated. He must have been thinking of the battle because he made a disgusted noise and shook his dagger at the swordsman.

"Put that sticker away, Grayf, and let me tell what a fool that Bigeln was. We were in this drinking hall finishing three or four small bottles. The townsmen are dirty, ugly and stupid—more animals than men. The only thing they care about is their stinking little god, N'tigh'ta. He's an ugly little monster with a big belly and a hollow head—they put sacrifices and such in this scooped-out top of his head.

They have little idols everywhere; it's about all you can do to avoid stepping on them."

Grant groaned as he turned his other side toward the flame.

"Well, we're sitting there drinking. That stupid Bigeln should have known better—he's been in this place before. But you know what he does? He's chewing weed, and before I can stop him, he rolls a great gob around on his tongue and lets fly."

Grayf, the other soldier, let his jaw drop with amazement.

"No!"

"Yes!" Aker roared the word out. "He thought the idol was a nice fancy little cuspidor. He spits in it, and those fur-pants' spowls let out a shout you can hear ten miles away. The next second we have our swords out and are fighting the whole damn town. They got Bigeln and I got out."

"But what about *this?*" Grayf jerked his thumb at Grant's collapsed form. "What are you going to do with him?"

Aker cut another slice of meat. "Not going to do anything with him. He was just standing around, so I brought him along to carry those hams. I warned to keep my sword arm free. Fact is, I don't even know who he is." He jabbed a giant thumb about three inches into Grant's ribs. "Hey—who are you?"

Grant opened one bleary eye and tried to gather together his foggy thoughts.

"M'name's Grant O'Reilly and I'm a student at Columbia. I was just...just standing...when..." He bogged down at the attempt to describe what had happened to him and his head dropped back onto his chest.

A pimple-faced boy of about sixteen, who had been keeping in the background, leaped forward, shouting at the same time.

"You heard him! He said he's a student—student magician, that's what! I'll cut his throat and drink his blood and take his clothes and—" He grabbed a handful of Grant's hair and snapped his head back, starting to draw a battered dagger across Grant's throat.

Aker shifted his weight and kicked the boy into a snowdrift.

"You take orders from me and that's all you do. You do the carrying and the cooking and leave him alone. Even if he is a student, he can fight, which is more than you can do." The boy drew back, sniffling and rubbing his hip, and threw a look of black malevolency at Grant.

Grant ignored him because he was already drifting into sleep.

CHAPTER FOUR

During the night, the flight and battle with the mob recurred in fragments of dream that wove in with what he had heard Aker Amen say; and slowly, penetrating ever deeper, with a chill like the cold beyond the fire, came the realization that these men spoke and lived as if their way of life was the only one—as if they had never heard of any other. Wherever his world of money, air-conditioned houses, of warm beds and swift automobiles and police and ambulances to protect him had gone, it was gone so unreachably far that Aker Amen and Grayf and the snarling ones in the tavern had never encountered it, never heard of it. However he had arrived here, he was a long way from home. There would be no easy road back.

Slowly through the night, the reality of memories of civilization and comfort and the hopes of rescue faded until they seemed mere fantasies of a world that had never been.

The boy poured water on the fire, and the hissing and steam woke Grant from his soggy sleep.

It was snowing again.

He felt mauled. His muscles ached terribly and were so stiff he could scarcely move. His back, which faced away from the fire, was numb with cold; his feet were soaked and his nose was running. He sat huddled beside the smoking ruin of the fire and tried to pull his ragged thoughts together. Perhaps he was in Alaska or some savage corner of Greenland. That was a possibility.

With his arms clasped around his legs and his chin resting on his knees, he was forced to stare at the tattered remains of his dress shoes. They focused his attention, because they were more than shoes. They were symbolic. The shoes were Grant. A well constructed, civilized product, perfectly in tune with a well-ordered world. Now a period of darkness and a night of madness, and that world was gone. Security and comfort vanished with it. All that remained of the shoes was a torn, bruised cover with a bit of blue flesh peeping through—his flesh. He rubbed his dripping nose on his coat sleeve and snuffled in self-pity.

It was still snowing, white flakes falling out of the gray lead sky into a silent world. The only thing he could hear was the soft sibilance of falling snow. Grant sat up suddenly, the little drifts of snow falling from his back.

The significance of the doused fire penetrated. He was alone.

He forgot the soreness and fatigue of his body now—it was a matter of survival again. Slipping in the slushy soup around the fire, he tottered to his feet. The clearing was empty. He screamed at the top of his lungs, his voice cracking with terror.

"Akerrrr...! Aker Amen! Helloooo!"

It was like shouting into a sea of drifting feathers, and produced as much result. He lurched around the clearing and noticed a track leading off through the trees. The footprints were fresh, but the windblown drifts were already beginning to fill them in. Grant followed them; it was his only chance for survival in this icebound wilderness. Aker would help him—*had* to help him. He realized for the first time how completely incapable he was. Without some help he would be dead by nightfall.

He pushed through the woods, stumbling over concealed obstacles and falling headlong in the drifts. As he came down a slight rise, he found himself on the same road-like track he had crossed on the way in. Three dimly seen figures were just starting up the bank on the far side. At his shout, they stopped and he rushed up to Aker, who was breaking trail.

"You can't leave—you can't leave without me! You've got to take me with you!"

Aker Amen adjusted his sword belt and fixed Grant with a cold, indifferent gaze.

"Why?"

Grant gaped twice, but couldn't think of what to say. There were no answers to the devastating question. Why should they help him? He realized instinctively that a plea of "humanity" or "friendship" would be worthless, as well as out of place. This society wasn't built like that. With the speed of desperation, his mind raced to other possibilities. Convenience, help? He knew that he didn't dare offer fighting assistance; last night had shown how woefully lacking he was in that important commodity. He could think of no other talents that might interest them. For the first time in his twenty-five years of existence he would have liked to reverse his civilized attributes and have a strong back and a weak mind.

Weak as his back was, though, it might be useful to them.

"I can carry your things, your equipment or whatever..."

Grant stopped suddenly as he realized that Aker and Grayf had, besides their weapons, only large leather wallets slung from their belts. His unspoken question was answered by a jerk of Aker's thumb.

Grant had been in such a panic when he passed the boy that he hadn't realized what he was carrying. He saw it now, a gigantic pack, hung with pots, sacks, and bundles and crowned with one of the stolen hams. The weight of this monster load had forced the boy to the ground as soon as the group stopped. He sat on a hummock in the road now, breathing heavily and greeting Grant with a malevolent stare.

That job was taken care of, too.

Aker Amen had turned back to resume the trail, but he stopped suddenly, his head cocked to one side. At the same instant Grant was aware of a distant rumbling, like muffled drums.

"Horses coming! Into the woods!" Even as he shouted the words, Aker was diving into the underbrush. Grant was too startled to act, but Grayf was galvanized into instant action. Grant was between him and the safety of the trees, a fact that made little difference to Grayf. He scarcely slowed when his shoulder hit Grant; then he was among the trees and Grant lay sprawled helplessly in a deep snowdrift.

The boy was still struggling to his feet when the horsewomen came. Grant had just a fleeting glimpse of them—long, flowing blonde hair and gilt breastplates—as they swept down the road. One of them uttered a coarse cry as they passed. She leaned far out of the saddle and made one sweeping stroke with her sword. The boy stumbled and fell to the ground. The ham, loosed by the fall, flew in one direction; the boy's head bounced in another. A thick stream of blood gushed from the dismembered neck and stained the snow a deep red.

The two soldiers reappeared at the edge of the road and hurled blistering oaths after the horses. Clear, girlish laughter floated back and they cursed the louder. Grant pulled himself from the chill embrace of the drift and tried to brush off most of the snow before it melted.

"You there—Grant O'Reilly! Still want to come along? We need a boy to carry our duffel."

Aker and Grayf howled with laughter and pounded each other on the back. Grant couldn't quite see the joke, and considered it to be in the worst taste possible. He found it hard, however, to stifle his own feeling of happiness and relief. The boy's death, untimely though it had been for the lad, might provide Grant's one chance of survival.

He pulled the pack straps from the limp form and tried to ignore the accusing stare of the bodiless head. He would have taken the pack and left, if Aker hadn't reminded him that survival was still the most important factor in this brutal world.

"Might as well take his clothes. Unless you have to wear those things you've got on."

Grant swallowed squeamishness and took the advice, while Aker Amen and Grayf waited, lounging against a tree and making remarks. The falling snow thinned and stopped as Grant stripped the boy's gray body, unpeeling layers of unsewn fur and belts and bands of leather that held the fur in place, and wrappings of filthy cloth which he dropped on the snow after he observed black specks of fleas hopping off.

Aker Amen shifted his weight with an impatient creak of leather. "Make it fast."

Grant could not grasp the intricacies of the boy's wrappings, but one large cowhide was slit in the center like a poncho, and when he slid his head through the hole and belted the hide around the waist with a leather strip from which dangled the boy's dagger, it was a neat, respectable tunic, and the thickness of the leather shut off the cold blasts of the wind. A sudden itch indicated the leather had other tenants, but just then he did not care.

Hastily, already feeling better, Grant sat down in the snow and ripped the soggy shoes off his blue feet, hissing between his teeth at the needling pangs they gave forth at every touch, and shoved them into the lumbering boots of the boy with a grunt that barely restrained desperate profanity.

The boots were warm and oddly soft inside and crackled when he stood up in them. He realized that they were mukluks, soft leather boots stuffed with hay. The Eskimos used them, he knew; his feet should be comfortable, though now they felt as if all the imps of hell were applying red-hot needles.

Bits and pieces of leather in various odd shapes were stacked beside the corpse in the snow. Grant looked them over uncertainly, draped one piece around his neck like a scarf, and took a piece that was wide in the middle and thin on the ends and tied it over his head and under his chin. Judging by Aker and Grayf's sudden roar of laughter, that was not the use for which the item was intended, but it kept the wind from his ears. Aker straightened, ready to go, and Grant abandoned the rest of the inexplicable odds and ends of leather and left them scattered beside the naked, headless body as he went to pick up the pack.

It was too heavy to get off the ground, but its shoulder straps stood out stiffly, as if suggesting a solution. He half knelt and slipped his arms through and then pulled himself hand over hand up a sapling until he was almost upright and had his legs under him enough to take his weight.

It was a neat bit of commonplace practical thinking, which he would not have been capable of a freezing half-hour ago. He was still cold, but he could move and think; his mind was no longer congealed with cold and already the exertion was beginning to warm him. He looked around for approval, but Aker and Grayf had vanished into the silent, snow-filled wood, leaving a double trail of footprints.

Stumbling under the unwieldy load, but moving ahead steadily, he followed the trail of the footprints, occasionally hearing the murmur of a voice ahead.

He was secure, with a place and a job and protectors. As he trudged, the exertion warmed him. His feet stopped flaming with thawing pains and began to feel like feet again. Without the counter-irritant of other aches for the first time, his attention was drawn to a hollow sensation in his stomach and he realized that he was hungry. As he walked he reached back with the dagger and hacked off slices of ham and stuffed them between his teeth. It was delicious in his salivating mouth; and once down, it glowed in his stomach, sending messages of nourishment and cheer through his blood. He ate enormously, although in a less hungry state he would have found the ham inedible. This time he had skipped three meals and had undergone more exertion than ever in any comparable period of his life. The badly smoked ham tasted like the best food he had ever eaten.

He was puzzled. By all that he knew about himself and his state of health, he should be feeling sick, or be dead, not feeling this unexpected exhilarated pleasure at the simple fact of eating; nor should he be enjoying the dazzling whiteness of snow in spite of the cumbersome weight of the pack he lugged. He had been told that he was weakly, that he should avoid exertion and excitement, yet he had the thought that no one who was weak could have picked up the monstrous pack at all. He had lifted it because he had to carry it or die, and every step was a new and conscious effort, but the strain was probably the effort to force lazy surprised muscles to do the job they had been intended to do, and the pangs were pangs of disuse.

Why had he ever believed he was an invalid?

Because his mother had told him, and because he had those fits of immobility.

Slipping and catching at bushes, he followed the trail of footprints as they wandered down an embankment and struck left along a dry creek bed at the bottom.

The floor of the creek bed was a nightmare for a novice woodsman. There were hidden tree roots to catch his feet and snow-laden branches to catch at his face and dump their burden of snow on his head. As he went on, he reviewed the passages in James Fenimore Cooper where the hunter went silently and skillfully through the forest, and remembered how he had envied and wished he could do it too. If he had followed his inclinations, he might have been as soft footed as an Indian, as magnificently muscled as Aker Amen, not a clumsy beginner.

His smooth-soled mukluks slipped on a downslopes in the streambed and he sprawled ignominiously on his back, and had to scrabble for holds to pull himself upright, losing many minutes before he could hurry on. Grant O'Reilly took the falls and bruises without the concern that had always made him fear mortal damage to his health—a bitter anger against his unused, pampered body kept him driving on. He would overtake Aker Amen and Grayf and show them he was no laggard.

But they remained elusive, although sometimes he heard their voices ahead. Hours passed, and as he went on, he remembered the coddling care his mother had given him, her warnings to avoid excitement, to stay away from the other children. Why had he believed her?

Because of the fits, the moments of dizziness and immobility. Yet now, when his muscles ran with liquid flame, when he had never exerted himself so much for so long in his life, he was not sick. Yesterday he had been closer to death and more legitimately frightened than at any time in his life, and yet he had had no fits and had not been sick. As a matter of fact, he felt more wide-awake and his senses were sharper now than at any time he could remember. Then what had given him fits and dizziness, if not this kind of thing?

Half kidding, half sliding down another short drop in the stream bed, Grant braced his hand against the bank and fell sidewise as his hand went through into a snow covered bush which had looked like solid earth. For a moment, in the sudden sheltering dark, he lay limp and thought of something that might be an answer. Excitement without any exertion was notoriously unhealthy, a source of ulcers to businessmen. And a child needed activity more desperately than an adult. Inaction, then, had made him sick. His mother's coddling had made him sick!

Anger drove him, and he clawed his way out of the bush and staggered out into the bright snowy day, to follow the footprints of the eternally elusive Aker and Grayf, grinding his teeth. He would show his mother, he would be a savage, like these savages, and not the puny, effete fool she had tried to make of him.

The soldiers held him in too much contempt to walk with him, he thought bitterly. They could tell he was following anyhow; probably the thumps and crashes of his blundering could be heard for miles. They did not know he had been deprived of his birthright, that he could have been as good a man as either of them, if he had been given a chance.

The sound of a branch cracking ahead and a murmur of voices encouraged him to totter forward at a more rapid rate. If only he could catch up, he might be able to ask them to stop for a short rest. He scrambled up a short embankment from the dry stream that they had been following and found the broken branch when he reached for the last handhold. There was no one there when he reached the top—only footprints which circled as if in doubt or discussion and then started off in a line again.

Grant followed, and the woods thinned and the ground grew more level. He could go faster now without tripping. He found himself stumbling across a large clearing and looked up from the trail of footprints just in time to see the two soldiers disappearing into the forest on the far side. He tried to make a cheerful shout, but the most noise he could muster was a faint croak.

But his voice was heard. He was answered from the woods behind his back by a rumbling cough that raised the short hairs on the nape of his neck!

There was terror in the sound, and a bestial strength that made him sick at heart. No animal he knew could make that sound and he had no desire to get better acquainted. He moved across the clearing as fast as he could. There was a crashing from the thicket he had left. His pace increased.

Halfway across the clearing he tried to look over his shoulder—and tripped. He sprawled in the snow. He could summon no strength to rise, even when the beast broke out of the woods.

At his first glance, it reminded him of a black kangaroo, but outside of the powerful rear legs there was little resemblance. The front legs were short and thick, ending in curved, white talons. The beast's head was long and wolfish the ears tufted like a lynx's, and very mobile. They twitched in all directions until they suddenly centered on Grant. The animal coughed again and then showed double rows of pointed teeth and charged.

Grant struggled to free his dagger as the beast bounded across the snow. He pulled it free of his belt but had no idea of how to use it on a brute each of whose paws held claws as long as his blade.

The black-furred legs sank into the snow six feet from where he lay. They contracted for a last leap. Grant could see the tiny green eyes, the saliva that speckled the black fur beneath the teeth.

There was a sudden *thunk,* the clean sound of an axe biting deep into a tree, and a feathered shaft appeared between the eyes. The legs jerked once and the great body flopped sideways, the black bulk half sinking into the white snow.

Grant looked dazedly at the lusterless eyes with the red arrow projecting between them. He looked quickly around. The forest was as quiet and apparently as empty of life as it had been all day. He shook once—and then again in an uncontrollable spasm. In the brief respite from walking, exhaustion had finally caught up with him and the delayed terror of death reached through his tired mind a second later. The woods were full of unseen black monstrosities and arrows of secret death.

He fought to his feet, struggling against the weight of the pack as if it were heavy paws on his shoulders and fled, screaming and staggering headlong through the forest. He would have run until he crashed into a tree if a strong arm had not stopped him.

Grant tried to struggle from the clutch, howling with terror, and at last freed himself of the pack. He did not feel the blow across his face—but he was sitting on the ground, the red mist clearing from before his eyes.

Then he saw that Aker Amen stood over him, and knew that he was safe. His body, racked by over-exhaustion, shook uncontrollably.

Aker Amen glowered down, and gauged Grant's buttocks with a not-too-gentle toe. "Now what's all the noise about? You hollered enough to be heard from here to the Crying Mountains."

"An animal," Grant stammered between deep gasps for breath. "Strange animal, black, big and black, with claws and long hind legs. It was going to—"

The description obviously meant something to Aker. He half drew his sword and peered into the thickets under the trees. "Damn the miserable luck! We've got a Berl-Cat on our trail. He must be right behind you."

Grant went white again and hastened to dismiss the idea. "No, the arrow took care of him, a perfect shot. But I couldn't see where it came from. That was the trouble." He was leaning on the ground, relaxing and letting his spine uncurl from the punishment of the pack load, quite sure that Aker Amen was woodsman enough to prevent any mysteries from creeping up on them. He was resting his eyes on Aker Amen's leather-wrapped feet as he talked, and he saw them suddenly stiffen motionless. It was an odd impression to get from feet.

Aker's voice reached his ears in a whisper. "What color was the arrow?"

"Red."

Grant looked up and saw sweat suddenly shining on the big soldier's forehead.

With a very slow, steady motion, his arms trembling with a barely perceptible tremor, Aker Amen put his left hand to his sword hilt and finished drawing it from its sheath.

"We have come in peace and we go in peace!" His voice was loud and falsely calm, and he seemed to be addressing the trees of the forest. "We love the holy men of Al'kahar, and desire to share the test of power."

Holding his sword dangling lightly from his fingertips, Aker pushed it carefully through the snow into the ground until it stood unsupported. He stepped away from it with a courteous gesture and hissed at Grant between his teeth. "Get up, you outland idiot! Slowly. Look *polite* and put your dagger in the snow."

Following instructions occupied Grant's attention. When he looked up, he saw the men coming out from between the trees...

They were coming from all directions. Men in black robes, their heads covered by cowls. Each man had a long red bow across his back and a handful of crimson arrows in his waistband. They crossed the snow as silently as falling leaves.

Their faces were the faces of the dead, gray and bloodless, with eyes that glimmered in the dark caverns of their eye sockets.

Grant tried to make out the expression in the eyes but if there had ever been a soul behind those eyes, that soul had died and rotted and dried up many years ago. It was like trying to look into the expression of a mummy.

Aker Amen's steady voice was like unexpected sanity in a bad dream. "I will give myself to the test of arm, and my companion will give himself to the test of..." He delayed and swept Grant with a contemptuous glance and muttered, "What in hell can you do? Sword, dagger, mace, bow...?"

Grant recalled that he had one talent that might be of value in this primitive place. He had taken archery, classified as a low exertion sport, for his required gymnasium credits in college. He heard his own voice, thin and hesitant.

"I think I could use one of those bows, if..."

Aker spoke loudly. "My companion will give himself to the test of eye. Who will test me?"

There was still no reply, but a black-robed figure, taller than the others, stepped forward and divested himself of arrows and bows. He pushed his hood back, revealing an expressionless head, as hairless, smooth and unhuman as a statue's head, with eyes no more alive than stone eyes.

Watching the man, Aker stripped off his weapons and armor and dropped them in the snow, leaving himself lightly clad and younger and more supple in proportions of shoulders to belly than Grant would have thought. Grant was again suddenly shamed with the realization that Aker was almost as young as he, for all his manly skills. The soldier stretched his muscles and arched his fingers, scanning his opponent, and estimating.

The others did not speak, even to murmur among themselves. The trees held the hush of snow-filled woods, and somewhere there was the susurration of an overladen fir branch bending and releasing its white burden to the snow covered ground.

The two men leaned forward imperceptibly; then like an uncoiling snake, in a blur of speed, the tall one in the dark cloak leaped forward with his spread fingers jabbing to

Aker's face. With equal speed, Aker slapped the hand aside before it reached him, as if slapping aside an insect and countered with an underhand swing of a balled fist. But the tall one's jab had been a feint and it was matched by a simultaneous low jab from the other hand. It might have killed a lesser man. Aker reacted with a startled grunt, and his first blow wavered off center, glanced off the other's ribs and spun the tall one away from him. The exchange of blows and jabs was short and fierce; it ended when the other hooked one of Aker's legs from beneath him. As Aker fell, he grabbed the other to him like a cat, twisted in midair and landed heavily with his opponent beneath him.

The robed stranger struggled to his feet with Aker on his back. They fell again, their feet kicked up streamers of snow, and again the tall one's tendoned hands crept over Aker's shoulders to seek his eyes. Aker buried his face against the other's back, muffling his eyes in the folds of the hood, and shifted position subtly. The muscles of his arms sprang up in clear relief and his tunic began to split across the shoulders.

For a moment they lay still, locked in ultimate effort, both of them so covered with snow as to be white sculpted marble; then a sudden small noise shot the length of the clearing, the sound of a dry branch cracking. Breathing heavily, Aker climbed to his feet and left his opponent lying limp with a broken spine.

Grant glanced around apprehensively, but the watchers remained impassive, without grief or vengeance for their dead companion.

Abruptly a bow and six arrows were shoved into Grant's hand. He looked at them stupidly until he heard

Aker Amen's fierce whisper. "Shoot, you fool! Hit some small target. Their man will have to match the shot."

With a heavy pounding in his heart, Grant set five of the arrows into his belt and nocked one onto his bowstring. The bow was heavier than the ones he was used to, and had a different feel. He would have liked to have had a few trial shots first, but knew that would be impossible. His hands were still trembling, but he hoped they would steady on the pull. Glancing around the clearing he saw a scar on a tall, oak-like tree. It was white against the dark trunk and should make an easy mark.

The bow had a very heavy pull. With great labor Grant drew the arrow back its full length and let fly. He almost gasped with horror as he saw it was a full six feet wide of the mark.

The arrow continued, arched downward, and struck a tree ten yards further on, impaling a sucker and pinning its single leaf to the bark. If that had been his mark, he would have considered it a good shot at an unusual distance.

The robed men had turned to follow the arrow's flight, and had not seen him wince at the miss. He tried to act smugly confident, in spite of the scowl and the fierce set of Aker's eyebrows. The soldier had been watching and was aware of Grant's ineptitude.

One of the dark figures moved next to Grant and pushed back his cowl. His hair had been shaved off and the pale skin was covered with small sores, even one with a tiny cut in the center. The sores were evenly spaced and, Grant realized with a shudder, undoubtedly self-inflicted.

The man wet his finger, tested wind direction, settled his feet, raised his bow, measured the distance and the mark a moment—then drew the string and released it in a single motion. The arrow was a scarlet blur against the leaden sky. It arched upward and fell straight hitting Grant's arrow and splitting a long sliver from it.

"Robin Hood," Grant tried to mutter sneeringly, but it did not succeed. Fear still clutched at his guts. Now the other would shoot first and Grant follow, and he had very little faith in his ability to best a marksman as sure and steady as the man with the sores.

His opponent nocked another arrow to the string and stood relaxed as one of the robed men poked into a coppice of small bushes.

The arrows were slid from Grant's belt as he watched. Startled, he glanced aside to see Aker standing close, peering at the arrows with his head bent ostentatiously.

"I think you were given crooked arrows—let me look at them." He stooped more closely over the arrows and Grant had a momentary glimpse of a bright flash in his hand. Aker had one of the arrows hidden behind the others and was rubbing it with something that flashed He whispered now, but Grant could catch the words.

"Sharp the point and keen the eye.
Hit the mark when off you fly."

He straightened up and handed the arrow to Grant.

"Here, this one looks to be the best."

When Grant examined the arrow, he started to smile. In his own crude way the barbarian was trying to help. Aker had scratched a little eye on the flat metal point of the arrowhead and muttered a spell over it! He had even daubed a little color onto it. Grant stared at the little green eye and it stared back.

Then it blinked slowly and looked away.

Grant jerked and almost dropped the arrow. He became aware with growing horror that the wood shaft was writhing gently in his hand. The point of the arrow was twitching back and forth. It reminded him of only one thing, a dog's nose twitching after a scent.

There was a swift whirring from the woods and Grant looked up, glad of the diversion. The beater had disturbed a covey of fat little birds and they flew up in a dun-colored cloud. Grant's opponent drew and shot with smooth speed, the red shaft hissing up. One of the birds was caught fair in the middle and tumbled down, impaled on the arrow. The men all looked to Grant.

He seemed to be watching himself also. He had the strange arrow nocked on the string and drawn back with no conscious effort. He never had the slightest chance to aim before his fingers relaxed and the arrow plunged upwards.

It hit one bird and, curving slightly, penetrated another bird. The weight of the two hapless flyers dragged at it and the arrow turned a slight arc and fell back towards earth.

The next thing was a little too grandstand, Grant felt, too much like showing off. The arrow turned obviously and impaled a squirrel to the branch it had been scampering along. Grant rubbed his eyes to clear away what he was sure was a fault of vision. When he looked back, the scarlet arrow was still stuck in the branch with its load of three tiny bodies. He had won the test of power by a score of three to one.

When the *whirr* of the flushed birds had faded away in the shadows under the trees, silence returned to the forest. The silence lasted an instant and was replaced by a sound.

The cry of a wounded cat, the throbbing wail of a coyote the trumpet of a bull elephant—these were the inhuman echoes of the sound, but there was more: the tone of sobbing, weeping, cursing, all the emotion-torn cries of sick mankind.

Heads back and mouths stretched wide as animals, the black-robed men wailed. Grant sank to his knees before it and covered his eyes against the rain of arrows he felt sure was to follow.

The wail throbbed and sank. He dropped his cowardly arm. A few bushes shook and were still. The clearing was empty. The dead man had been carried away. The heavy beating of his heart and the bow and arrows tightly clutched in his white-knuckled hands were the only signs of the strangers' visit.

Aker Amen had also felt the terror of that last wail. He pulled his sword from the snow and cursed eloquently as he wiped the blade dry. Grant walked to where he had dropped his pack and collapsed against it. Without interrupting his stream of invective, Aker aimed it at Grant.

"You misbegotten, worm-fingered, stew-brained, rock-headed civilian...if you hadn't made all that fuss with the Berl-Cat those Al'kahar maniacs might never have heard us. Not only that, but with your lousy shooting I had to use up that good *climean* spell! Urrrgh..." The vituperation tapered off into a growl of anger as he buckled on his armor. As soon as all his equipment was secured, he started to leave, but turned to glare at Grant tugging tiredly and half-heartedly at the pack. "Rouse up and lean into that pack—we have to be out of these woods by sunset."

He did not say why, but Grant needed no urging. He had his fill of the things that lurked in this forest.

He lifted the hand clutching the bow and arrow, nodding questioningly at the encircling forest.

"Keep 'em," Aker growled. "You're supposed to have won them." He started moving again. With a certain confidence at having a weapon at last, Grant unstrung the bow and shoved it and the arrows into a strap of the pack and shrugged the giant burden onto his shoulders. By the time Aker reached the edge of the clearing, Grant was a pace behind, settling the burden into position as he went.

Suddenly he was aware that Grayf was missing, and had been missing through the entire affair. Between shifts of the pack he wheezed, "Where's Grayf?"

"We were down the trail when I heard your noise. I came back. He should have gone ahead and waited." And Aker Amen added like a grim prayer, "If he went far enough away he'll be out of the way of *them.*"

Five minutes later a turn of the trail gave them the answer. Grayf lay there face down, his arms extended and his fingers hooked into the ground. He was like a monstrous pincushion full of monstrous red pins. From his back and legs there projected at least two dozen arrows.

"The fool must have tried to run." Aker passed the body in a wide circle, dragging Grant after him. "Don't go near him, or you'll look the same. The dead are sacred to the Al'kahar." He added in a fierce rumble, "That's what they eat."

As soon as they were out of sight of the riddled corpse Grant leaned against a tree and tried to lose his breakfast.

CHAPTER FIVE

They continued the next hours at a slower pace. Aker grumbled and prodded Grant on with word and toe, but soon gave up and adapted his stride to that of the slower man, frequently ranging ahead silently to scout the trail.

At dusk they came to the end of the forest. The trees ended abruptly at the edge, a vertical escarpment, a granite wall with a thread of trail meandering down the face of it, widening out once into a green tree-grown shelf, then narrowing again. At the foot was a pleasant valley, with fields and meadows, and far away a smudge of smoke rising from some kind of habitation.

As they went down the path they left the forest of the "holy men" of Al'kahar.

The path was less difficult than it had looked from above; it had been hand carved many ages ago, to judge from the weathering, but it was still usable and steps had been hacked out for the worst descents. The brisk wind swept the path free of snow. Grant concentrated on balancing his pack and staying away from the sheer drop on his left.

There was a shallow grotto where the trail leveled off halfway down, and the smoke-blackened wall and lumps of charcoal under the snow showed that travelers had stopped here before. As Grant groaned out of his pack, Aker ranged ahead onto the shelf with its overgrowth and the sound of wood being hacked rang back. The long sword had more than one use.

Now that they had stopped, Grant's hard-earned warmth seeped away. He hopped from one foot to another and blew on his numbed fingers.

Aker was back after a time with a load of dead branches. He stamped a clear spot at the base of the stone wall, where the stones before it would cut off the light of the fire, and made a conical pile of broken sections of tree limb. Then he shredded a mound of splinters under them. From the depths of his wallet he dragged out a small metal box. Grant guessed that it contained a fire bow, or flint and steel. He was taken aback when Aker shook a little orange lizard out into his hand. The lizard, sluggish from the cold, slowly drew the nictitating membrane from one eye. Obviously unhappy at the frigid world, it closed the membrane and tried to curl up. Aker stirred it to life with a blunt finger and proffered a few splinters picked from the freshly cut wood. This unlikely food seemed to please the little reptile; its eyes flew open and it gulped the splinters down. It chewed voraciously when Aker produced some larger splinters about the size of toothpicks.

Grant was annoyed and cold. He couldn't see the connection between playing with the pet and starting the much-needed fire. The lizard, finished with his dinner, began to curl up again and go back to sleep. Aker brought it close to the mound of splinters and squeezed its tail. The lizard gave him a protesting roll of its eyes and belched a small cloud of flame. Aker popped it back into its box and blew on the smoldering kindling.

Grant felt his mouth hanging open stupidly. In fairy tales he remembered mention of a creature something like this. The mythical lizard that lived on flame. "A salamander!" he murmured aloud.

"Yeah," Aker mumbled between blasts at the fire. "They come in real handy."

CHAPTER SIX

The snow had stopped and the wind had fallen at sunset. The fire roared and sizzled and threw back a warm glow from the rock wall. Grant's stomach ground contentedly. He pulled a piece of gristle from between his teeth with a grimy forefinger, surprised he could actually be feeling so well. His body was exhausted, but he enjoyed the pleasure of relaxation after continued exertion. He took a long drag of sour wine from the musty animal-skin container.

He had the salamander box open and teased the little animal with a twig. The indignant lizard blew out a little cloud of red flame, but he jerked his fingers away in time. He fed it some tender splinters to soothe its ruffled feelings. It chewed the wood contentedly and let a little trickle of smoke out of its nostrils.

The tiny lizard symbolized all his troubles. By the laws of reality it couldn't exist. Neither could these strange people with their impossible customs, nor the Berl-Cat, nor the spell that Aker had used on the arrow. Either he was insane and this world was all a part of his tortured mind; or, if he were sane, he had been transported here from his own world in some unthinkable manner. Wherever *here* was.

"Aker, what country is this?"

"Ter-Klosskrass, Independent Free State of the Tyrant Helbids, Na'tunland. What's the matter, you lost or something?"

"Something." Grant went back to tugging at the gristle between his teeth. The names meant nothing to him. *The names*—they weren't English; yet Aker spoke perfect English. Well, maybe not perfect—but crude English. This must be the key to the key to the whole mess.

"Aker, how is it that you speak perfect Xtylporf...I mean Hiiopmert..." Grant stopped and rubbed the sudden perspiration from his forehead. Aker looked up from his sword-sharpening operation, slightly startled.

"How come I speak *what?*"

Grant knew what he wanted to say; the concept was perfectly clear. The English language, tongue of our fathers, Shakespeare, literature courses at Columbia. The English language. He'd say it slowly this time...ENGLISH!

"UZQINNP!"

"You better give me the wine skin. I think you need some sleep."

"No, no. Aker, you must listen! Haven't you ever heard of...my country? The capitol city is Rtyydbx, I live in..." Grant didn't say it, he didn't want to hear it. He knew he would say something horrible that didn't sound in the slightest like New York. He could visualize the ideas so clearly, but he didn't have the words to express himself.

Was it amnesia? Or was it, the thought struck him suddenly, that he was no longer speaking English?

"What language are we speaking?"

"Why, High Na'tunlish of course. Are you stupid—or trying to kid me that you don't know the name of your own language? I can tell you were born here—no accent like me." He gave his chest a thumping blow. "I'm pure Inin tribesman. Slave traders stole me when I was a boy. I killed them later and became a Free Soldier. That's when I first learned Na'tunlish, so I still got an accent. Not like you."

Grant O'Reilly knew he had not been born here. He was sure now that *here* was not even his own world. This must be another world altogether, separate from his own in time and space. He wasn't sure about the details—it had been a long time since he had read H. P. Lovecraft—but this theory seemed the most tenable.

It also explained the language difficulties—or lack of difficulty. He spoke the language of this world, or this part of the world. Sort of like turning a radio to a different station. Same tubes and parts, but a different frequency going in, so different words came out. It was as if he had been tuned out of his own world into this one. The words for *English* and New *York* did not exist here; only their abstract concepts existed in his brain. It was all very confusing.

The wine and the warmth of the fire were making his head heavy. He pulled what looked like a moth-eaten bearskin rug out of the pack and wrapped it around himself. There was another question he wanted to ask. He raised his head and opened his eyes.

"Aker, who were those men in the forest?"

The soldier growled deep in his throat like a big cat and spat into the fire. "Al'kahar ghouls! They're the curse of these filthy woods. They *test* all the travelers they can lay their hands on and eat all the ones who fail the test. Something to do with their religion." He spat again, as if to rid his mouth of an unpleasant taste. "There are more of them in the valley, but we'll be out of their territory in the morning."

By heroic effort of will, Grant kept himself awake long enough to arrange the bearskin comfortably so that only his nose was sticking out; then, muffled and warm, he fell into dreamless sleep.

CHAPTER SEVEN

In the morning it was raining. Rain dripped steadily from the mouth of the shallow cave, making long soggy looking icicles that fell off with a crash, leaving the dripping rock bare for the formation of more icicles.

The fire had gone out and the warmth long departed from the rock. The damp reached up from the sodden ground through the worn animal skin that covered Grant and drew the warmth from his body. He pried open gummy eyes and stared at the dawn sky, gray and dripping. He tried to go back to sleep, but Aker must have heard his movements. A prehensil toe reached out and gouged him in the most sensitive part of his chilled anatomy.

"Get up and start the fire." The voice was muffled, but the meaning was clear. Grant groaned as he hauled his stiff form out of the covers.

The salamander burnt his finger instead of lighting the fire, and he pinched its tail in retaliation. He found a small log, back in a crevice of the cave, and dropped it on his toe and cursed with a growing fluency for at least ten minutes. In spite of this the fire was finally started, and Aker Amen pulled himself next to it and heated up a slab of ham. Grant followed suit, then turned back into his blanket and shivered with comfort, glad that it was raining. There was no going out into the icy rain and Grant wondered, if there had been no rain, *could he have picked up the pack and continued?* He answered himself. *No!*

After breakfast, Aker hummed a war song as he cleaned the matted blood and hair from the spikes of his mace, and told a few reminiscent tales of the skulls the mace had crushed. The rain continued, so he went on with each of his weapons and pieces of armor in turn, telling the stories they reminded him of as he cleaned them. The life of a free soldier was close to the life of a bandit, Grant decided as he listened. It was a carefree sort of telling, but incredibly villainous by civilized standards.

He crawled closer to the fire and wrapped himself more tightly in the blanket. Every joint creaked with the motion, and though he was almost as hot as a toasting ham slab, he continued shivering in spasms.

"You sick?" Aker eyed him sharply.

Grant came out with an excusing lie he had thought of to explain his faults, a lie that he considered more than half true. "No, just out of condition. Weak, I was…a prisoner a long time and I've gotten soft." He paused, ashamed but pleased by the respectful attention visible in Aker Amen's face, then added with a burst of worried truth. "I can't see why I keep shivering. I'm not cold."

"Stiffening up," Aker said casually, "If you don't keep moving around you'll be as stiff as a timber brace by morning," He chuckled, and reached a long arm for a branch from the depleted fire stick. "When you come back from collecting firewood, we'll have a little sword practice."

With every muscle creaking in protest like a rusting puppet, Grant dragged himself out of his blanket to look for firewood in the cold rain. When he came back, drenched and shivering, Aker greeted him with a blow of a light stick he had fashioned from a branch, and handed Grant another to defend himself with. Aker amused himself by swinging slow motion blows at Grant and watching him scramble clumsily to parry or duck.

Thus the day passed and it was probably the rain that gave Grant a chance to live and survive, for it rained the next day, too, and in the alternate drowsing by the fire and being prodded awake to seek firewood, in listening open-mouthed to Aker Amen's good-natured tales of thievery, rapine, loot and death, he gradually recovered from the exhaustion and cold-shock of the two days before. The shudders stopped, the weakness and stiffness passed and he ate more ravenously than ever in his memory, the meat going to fill some insatiable hollowness within.

Even as early as the second day, the thin muscles over his big-boned frame had begun to thicken, responding eagerly to the strains that, after a delay of years, had come to them as a cue for growth.

Grant did not appreciate the process; he only wanted to sleep and eat; and yet he had to busy himself collecting firewood. He picked up numerous small bruises around head and throat to the tune of Aker Amen's roaring laughter, until he learned to fend off the unexpected blows from the light stick in Aker Amen's hand. He was learning the elemental skills of handling a broadsword.

The muscles of his wrist and arm and shoulder were alerted by this unaccustomed stress and put in their share of call for more nourishment.

At the end of the second evening, Grant and Aker finished the remains of the second ham, and, for a tidbit, ate a squirrel, which Grant had put an arrow through in the afternoon. The rain stopped and only the sound of dripping and running water was heard, and the air began to chill.

"Tomorrow we move," growled Aker, and put his sword carefully beside him as he lay down to sleep, for with the rain stopped, the predators of the night would be abroad again.

"Where are we going?" Grant's question was muffled by the warm bearskin.

The other man had rolled up next to the fire. He raised his head for an instant, light from the fire glinting from his eyes. "We're going to a war of course, what else? It's going to be good. Wine and blood. Kill and be killed. Good, huh?"

The philosophy of these barbarians could not have been better expressed. Grant roused himself just long enough to answer, with a wry glimmer of irony. "Good, sure...that's the only way to live—die." He sank back into a dreamless sleep.

The fire crackled and died. The only sound was the dry rustling of the dead leaves in the trees. The clouds blew away and the stars pierced the cold winter sky, sharp and diamond-like.

CHAPTER EIGHT

The next morning was clear and cold. Grant got up first without any prodding and, shivering, broke the stacked firewood free from the iced ground, and made a small fire. Aker sat up and began humming a battle chant as he buckled on his armor and hung his weapons at his belt.

The sight of the wicked instruments plus the memory of the past four days of bloodshed tended to make Grant thoughtful as he stowed away the contents of the giant pack. The idea of putting on that pack again merely to go murder or be murdered hardly seemed worth the struggle. If he were separated from Aker Amen he would not have to carry all that baggage.

The thought came to him with a twinge, for he liked the big soldier, and had a hunch the soldier liked him—that the rough treatment he was getting, by the standards of these people, was an extreme of good-natured protection.

The big soldier finished stowing away his deadly arsenal and kicked the fire down into the snow. "Let's go."

Grant stood up beside the pack and cleared his throat. "Er...Aker...I've decided to try some other way of life...I mean...I'm not so good as a fighter. You don't need me along."

His big decision made no observable difference to Aker. The soldier hooked a giant hand through one of the pack-straps and lightly swung it across his shoulder.

"Fine by me, only watch out for Berl-Cats. And Holy Men. The woods are full of them. And if you get clear of the woods, don't go near the peasants. They don't like strangers. If they catch a stranger they stick a big sharp pole through his bottom and stand him out in the fields to dry out for a scarecrow."

The last words were a little indistinct as Aker was trudging off rapidly down the trail. Grant, who always had a pictorial mind, felt his anal sphincters twinge. He quickly followed.

Aker turned at his hail and dropped the pack on the ground, then went on without slowing his pace. With an inward groan, Grant slipped the straps into the well-worn grooves on his shoulders and found—with surprise—that the burden was not nearly as heavy as he had expected. Perhaps because of the peculiarly vivid alternative Aker Amen's remark had conjured up, but more likely because the ham was now eaten and gone. Grant thought he saw a tilt to the back of Aker's head, which meant a big grin was on the front of it.

The trail wound out of the trees to the edge of the cliff again and steepened, going down its face toward the trees of the valley.

At the last turning, Aker suddenly became wary. "This place stinks like an ambush, I'll see what's below."

With Grant standing back and covering him with a necked arrow, Aker spent a seemingly interminable time crawling up to the edge of the cliff with a branch in front of his face and peering down. Apparently satisfied, he crawled back, then went a little way down the bend of the trail.

Grant slipped the pack off his back and stretched his shoulder muscles. Nothing moved below. Aker had stopped on a little ledge and was again peering into the depth below.

Grant yawned, and turned his head automatically at a slight movement to his right, then went rigid as one of the hideous Berl-Cats came out of a cave.

It had not seen him yet, but he could see the nose and whiskers twitching, following some scent. There was a clink of metal from the trail below. The beast looked up alertly, the ears turned in the direction of the sound. With one bound, it was at the edge. Aker was on the edge twenty feet below, his road back turned helplessly toward the animal.

With utmost silence, Grant raised his bow. The string was taut and he was sighting down the arrow as the animal's legs tensed to leap. The range was short and the twang of the bowstring and the chunk of the arrow came as one sound. The cat made a small mew of pain as its foreleg was pinned to its ribs. It had leaped as he fired.

Grant saw a perfect example of the reflexes needed to survive in this barbarian world. At the sound of the bowstring, Aker's head had jerked up, and at the sound of the cat's cry, the big man in the leather armor leapt back and had his sword out and braced, blade slanting up, ready to impale anything that landed on him.

If the big cat had landed on Aker, it would have been spitted. It tried hard to do just that, but it could not change its course in mid-leap. Snarling and twisting and clawing towards him in the air, it passed through the spot where Aker had been, caught with its good foreleg on the edge of the drop, was over-balanced by the failure of its wounded foreleg, and twisted with an outraged mewling over the edge. There was a crash and a sound of rolling and sliding and scrabbling down through the brush.

Aker wiped the hilt of his sword before returning it to his scabbard, and looked up at Grant with more respect than before. "A fair shot, Granto." He waved Grant after him and moved towards the valley.

With caution, alert for the wounded cat, they filed down the path to the trees.

The snow began again, and soon filmed everything in white. The woods ended at the edge of a cleared field and they climbed an embankment onto a rutted farm road. The road swung through the fields and passed close by a sod-covered stone house.

Grant watched it nervously and found his suspicions justified as four bearded men, followed closely by a shrieking woman, ran through the doorway. They howled crude obscenities and swung a wicked assortment of flails and scythes over their heads. It was a startling sight, and Grant flinched back. Aker seemed to find it neither frightening nor interesting. He stood quietly, a bored sneer on his lips, as they approached.

The screaming men were just a few yards away when he whipped out his long sword and bellowed a terrible war cry. The great weapon flashed just once, and the flails of the first pair were hacked in two. They stared stupidly for a long instant and then fled, howling a more despondent note this time. Long before they had resumed the safety of the house, Aker had turned his back and continued his interrupted course down the road.

The episode reminded Grant again of the value of swordsmanship. He picked up a stick and, as he trudged down the road, swung at every mark that caught his eye, trying to learn to gauge a swing from any angle to hit the spot precisely, imagining the spot as an enemy. It made the time pass entertainingly, and again he felt that sharpening of the senses, almost exhilaration, that seemed to have something to do with the steady exercise and something to do with the clean whiteness of the landscape and much to do with a feeling of irresponsibility.

They stopped at noon by a frozen stream and made a lunch from an unspeakable lump of bread dredged from the depths of the pack. Aker kicked a hole in the ice and they mixed a drink in the horn cups—half spring water and half wine. It was an invigorating and thirst-quenching drink, particularly since the water seemed to be carbonated and flavored. Grant smacked his lips over it and made no attempt to understand the geological impossibility that produced it.

The road wandered up the wide valley and they stuck to it, rather than cut across the furrowed fields. About mid-afternoon the winter ended.

That was the only way that Grant could describe it. They trudged along the road, ankle deep in the snow, with the big flakes falling slowly on all sides. The sky seemed much lighter ahead, and then Grant noticed what appeared to be a line drawn across the road. The near side of the road was covered with snow, but beyond the line the warm sun shone on the brown dirt road and green fields. They passed the invisible barrier with no difficulty but, on looking up, Grant saw that none of the snowflakes were getting through. The ones that approached simply vanished.

On three sides stretched a warm and fertile landscape; behind was a wall of whirling flakes and a frigid winter scene. Grant looked at it dumbfounded.

Sunshine and a warm breeze seemed to please Aker. He opened the collar of his jerkin and took a deep breath of the grass and tree-scented air.

"Were getting close to the army. It's good to feel a little on the back. That's why I always like to work for the Good Duke Darikus—he's got gout and stand cold weather. The sun always shines on Darikus. That's what they say."

"You mean he's *causing* this warm weather?"

"Sure. He casts a mean spell. Built this one up twenty-five years ago, I hear. Hasn't failed yet. It's always mid-summer around him, no matter what the weather should be."

They had topped a rise in the road and before them lay a green meadow bright with tents and pavilions and dark with the figures of many men. Most of them wore leather or chain armor; a few, mounted on the six-legged horse-like animals, wore full armor of silver and gold. The air was filled with the murmur of many voices, of shouted orders and the clank of steel and sound of bugles. A guard tent stood close by the road, a half dozen pike-men lounging around it.

The nearest soldier sighted Grant and Aker. He leveled his pike across the road and challenged them in a sleepy voice.

"Halt and be recognized. What business here?"

"Free Soldiers to serve the Good Duke Darikus."

Satisfied, the soldier lowered his weapon and shouted toward the tent.

"Hey, Corporal, couple more guys want to join up."

There was a stirring in the tent and a young man with a long, curling mustache poked his head out. He looked the two men over with an insulting stare. His gaze fixed on Grant's sagging form and scanned the indoor pallor and the gentle look that was part of the blondness of his hair and eyebrows. The corner of the man's mouth turned back in a sneer.

"Looks like pretty poor material, but I suppose you better take them to the Duke—he'll hire anybody."

Aker spat full in the man's face and loosened his sword in the scabbard.

"Right you are, sonny, he hired *you*. I was fighting with the Good Duke when you were still peeking under your nurse's skirt." Aker started to walk away but turned and added, as a happy afterthought, "Want to fight?"

The corporal wiped his beet-red face and opened and shut his mouth like a fish out of water. He looked more closely at Aker this time. He saw the man's tremendous girth and mighty arms under the travel-stained leather and thought twice. His head popped back into the tent. The soldiers grinned happily and a pair detached themselves to go with Aker and Grant.

They made their way through the camp and up to the largest tent, a sprawling construction of many-colored cloth. A pennant flew over the entrance, a black, mailed fist squeezing out drops of blood against a white field. The pikemen saluted the flag. Grant and Aker saluted also, then entered the tent.

Armed soldiers stood around the walls. Two littered tables stood in the center; a thin clerk with ink-stained fingers sat at one, an old man wearing a gold coronet sat at the other. Aker stepped forward and saluted with a thump of his fist against his chest.

"Hail, Duke. I am here to serve you."

"Hail, hell. Who are you and what's *that* with you?" the Duke replied testily, and shifted his bandage-wrapped foot on its cushion.

"Aker Amen and spear slave."

Grant started to protest his new status but closed his mouth when he realized that Aker undoubtedly knew best how to handle the situation. The affair with the corporal of the guard proved that. The clerk was rapidly flipping pages in a giant, leather-bound book. He ran his finger down one page and then read from the selected line.

"Amen, Aker, born Inin, Master Swordsman, Axe Expert, Excelling Infighter, qualified on dirk, mace, arbolest, crossbow, scimitar…"

"All right!" The Good Duke interrupted him. "Two gold *Enn* a day, and loot for you, loot for the slave and pick of the captured weapons. Done?"

"Done," Aker roared. "We fight to the death!" He slammed the flat of his hand down on the table, signifying his acceptance of the contract. The Good Duke slammed his down too and winced as the vibrations shook his gouty foot. Grant wondered if he should slam also, but Aker turned and pushed him out of the tent.

More men milled about. Grant saw why when they formed a ragged line leading to a giant stew kettle. He and Aker joined the end of the line. As they shuffled forward he thought over the recent past, then turned to Aker.

"You never told me—who are we going to fight?"

"I don't know. What difference does it make? Get some chow, you're next."

When they each had a horn cup full of steaming stew and were finishing it off as they walked along, looking for tent space, Aker spoke again with his mouth full. "Ask an officer. He might know."

"Maybe later." Grant walked, absorbing the sun warmth and the rich mingled flavor of meats and potatoes and rice and unidentified vegetables. He was beginning to accept Aker Amen's philosophy. "Not a bad stew."

CHAPTER NINE

The Duke was planning to attack the Tyrant Helbida, whoever that was. The fifth man Grant asked told him that much, but no one knew when they would attack, not even the Good Duke himself. According to the talk of the camp, every evening at sundown His Goodness cast a pair of twelve-sided astrological dice onto a silken cloth. So far the omens and portents of the dice had not been favorable for the morrow, so the army stayed in the encampment, eating and guzzling, lounging and quarreling, and polishing up on the arts of slaughter.

Twice a day, everyone turned out to the drill field, the soldiers and officers rounding up all the reluctant novices and conscripts that could not escape, and herded them to the field where they hammered away at each other with an earsplitting rattle and clamor. The experienced soldiers worked out against each other with live steel; beginners and those less competent were given wooden swords and poles for spears.

The novices were prevented from leaving the field during drill, but otherwise were not watched, so Grant transferred himself from the spearmen to the group learning the broadsword. The reluctant beginners belabored each other, sweating and bruised, often angry and cursing, urged on by shouts from the officers. Grant found quickly when a parry was poor by picking himself up from the dust. But he husbanded his strength, put brains into his fighting, was watchful of techniques and thought about his mistakes when he picked himself up and he kept at the practice in the after hours when most of the others left the field.

In a few days Grant sported a mask of colorful bruises and lumps, and a vastly improved fighting technique. Aker Amen, strolling over after working out with the swordsmen, sometimes separated Grant from his novice opponent and picked up a wooden sword to give Grant a few painful but useful demonstrations of professional swordsmanship.

The fifth day a new element was added. For the entertainment of the professional soldiers and the officers who lined up on the sides, shouting encouragement and making bets, the end of the afternoon's drill was turned to a free-for-all. The trainees were turned loose on the field with instructions to fight, and keep fighting until disarmed or unconscious. The only rule was to keep the combat single combat still, but the rule was not enforced. Broken bones and missing teeth were in evidence from the moment the fray started.

One group of thickset louts, obviously farm conscripts, were the terror of the field; they stuck together, attacking in such close sequence that no outsider had time to collect his scattered wits between one bout and another. Soon their end of the field was scattered with the defeated, and a wide clear space was being given them by the others. Their leader was a young giant named Splug, who seemed to be beating down everyone he encountered by sheer weight and strength and fatness.

Grant tried to stay to one side and fight a quiet defensive fight without attracting attention to himself, but this time he had an appointment with destiny. He was due to find out something about himself, a fact he had kept hidden for an entire lifetime.

Splug saw him from the distance and shouted, then charged with a roar of laughter, evidently deceived by Grant's mild expression and unassuming stoop.

Slobbering, he swung a simple overhand blow down at Grant with the clumsy simplicity of chopping wood. Grant parried it easily and thumped the other in the ribs on the return stroke. Angered, Splug swung again with tremendous force and weight, his muscles standing out under his fat. Grant's guard held, but by sheer push, he was forced to give ground. Stepping back, he found a wooden sword tip inserted between his feet, tangling them, and lost balance. One of the other farm hands was slyly helping his leader. As Grant tottered, Splug cracked him across the head and roared with laughter. When Grant stepped away from the entanglement and tried to return the blow, a foot tripped him from another direction, and the wooden sword hit his shoulder with a white burst of pain. Splug laughed again.

At that moment Grant felt one of his fits coming on. The ringing began in his ears and the pressure in his temples and the distance from sounds. Why now, of all times?

The brutes were all around him, all wide and sturdy, and enough alike to be brothers, probably conscripted from the same inbred farm town. They all worked together; if Grant fell they would probably beat and trample him into the ground, the officers couldn't see what was happening. He had to fight.

He felt as if he were growing. Everything else seemed small and clear and the wooden sword seemed as light in his hand as a matchstick. The blows he received felt light and distant and the blows he struck seemed like taps. He swung countless taps at things that looked like Splug, or perhaps the same tap over and over; it was all the same. But through the distance, he was aware that he was enjoying himself. He felt relaxed! There was no resistance either inside or outside, as in a dream.

Then startlingly, everything went black. He came up to the surface again, sitting on the ground, holding his aching head in both hands. An officer was standing over him, slapping a weighted cosh into the palm of his hand thoughtfully. He scowling as Grant looked up.

"Just keep your temper after this, me lad. We're here for practice, not for skull cracking."

Grant looked around dazedly at a circle of unconscious figures. Splug was a distance away, sitting up, holding his bloody face and moaning. Across the field the other fighters had stopped and were watching Grant. The entire thing made no sense.

The officer said, "You had reason enough. They were asking for trouble. But when you started to ram the broken end of your sword down the fat one's throat you were asking for trouble. I had to tap you one. Just try to save that kind of thing for the enemy from now on."

Looking around with slowly dawning understanding, Grant saw that all the men were Splug's gang. A few were beginning to crawl painfully to their feet and stagger away.

He felt himself blush. "I beg your pardon. I didn't mean to..."

"I don't say you didn't give fair warning, howling like that," grinned the officer. "But try to hold your temper down next time."

The grizzled bear-like man walked away, his gold armor glinting, but Grant stood up slowly, thinking of what he had been told—that he had a hot temper!

This was a thing he had never known. What he had been calling fits, and thinking of as illness, was temper, a hot, sudden wish to kill, too primitive for thought, too savage for civilized expression. It was too strange for recognition as part of the Grant they had always called a sweet boy, and a little angel—or later a sensitive type. Finding no outlet of action or thought for the emotion, he had had fits, rigid and shaking, with his mind a blank until the anger passed.

This time the temper had found outlet. He spun slowly on his heel, surveying his victims. The thought occurred that there might be a berserker, among his ancestry. From the Swedish side of his family, he had inherited his blond hair and almost white brows. He could have inherited his disposition also. The ancient Swedes were the people who occasionally produced berserkers, men of apparently gentle disposition who, in battle, changed and killed as savagely and blindly as uncaged tigers.

He stood there in the torn field, looking gentle and worried, not as skinny as before, but still a slim, tall figure with a scholar's stoop and a delicate look. Yet none of the others sneered at his slumped figure, and they left a wide space around him as they returned to their fighting.

He swung the broken sword in an idle pattern as he walked off, badly worried with the wonder of how close he had been the other times during his life. How near had he been to committing murder when he thought he was just being sick?

The next fit came just two nights later. He and Aker had been drinking late in a tent across the camp. They were weaving back, leaning on each other and singing one of the plaintive melodies of this world. Aker sang the verses and Grant came in, loud and flat, on the chorus.

She told the king no, but smiled at me
And lifted her dress above her pink knee.
I said, why bless me, I never did see
Such a...

A dark figure stepped out from behind a tent and landed a heavy blow on the back of Aker's head. The big soldier dropped, the breath whooshing from his limp body, and simultaneously Grant was backhanded to the ground by a gloved fist, his uncertain balance easily destroyed.

The man stepped out into the moonlight and Grant recognized the mustached corporal of the guard, on duty the day he and Aker arrived.

"Nobody spits in my face," the man muttered, and raised his foot to grind it down on Aker's face. As a burst of icy distance and rage shot through his brain, Grant swung his wooden sword up across the corporal's throat as if, by hatred, the wood had become a real sword. It seemed a light blow, but the man began to crumble together, then hunched over and poured blood out of his mouth as from a tilted bottle, and continued bending more and more until he folded down onto the ground, a shrunken and writhing bundle, rapidly becoming still. Grant stared numbly until he remembered he had heard of the deadly trick of breaking the larynx. Apparently he'd done it.

As Grant pulled himself to his feet, he became aware for the first time that someone else was there. The flap on a lighted tent had been thrown back and a man stood there watching. From the rings that flashed on his fingers, he must be a noble of some kind. He laughed suddenly, and Grant recognized him—the officer who had knocked him out on the drill field.

"Remember what I said, about controlling your temper."

He noticed Grant's tense position and laughed again. "Don't worry, I'm not going to turn you in. Anyone who hits a man in the midst of a good song deserves what he gets. Drag your friend in here and pour some wine down his throat. I want to hear the rest of that verse. I thought I knew all of them!"

He turned back for an instant. "Bring the body in too. The armor and weapons are yours by right of conquest, anyone who can kill with a wooden sword deserves a man's weapon."

The next day Grant swaggered through the camp in leather armor with a bow and quiver of arrows slung on his back and the weight of a light broadsword at his belt. He enjoyed the way the servants and slaves of the camp scurried out of his path, the deference they gave a fighting man, and noticed the eyes of the women camp followers turning to him as he went by.

Then he felt something like a fool as he carefully took off his armor at the practice field and picked up a wooden sword to practice with. He showed himself no more strong or skilled than the day before when he had been merely ranked as a slave. But he lost himself in the exercise and the day passed quickly. At the dinner call, Grant grounded his sword, suddenly aware of weariness, but aware he had learned and improved.

He went to buckle his armor back on. After only one day it was beginning to feel like a second skin and he had felt naked without it.

Aker went by with the stream of men heading for the stew line and slapped him on the shoulder as he passed, which he had been doing often since Grant had won his armor, his way of expressing his pleasure in what had happened.

At the meal line the word was passed. The cast of the Duke's dice had been favorable. Tomorrow they would fight. There was a rush of last minute readying of weapons, and a blowing of discordant bugles for formations.

CHAPTER TEN

They marched in the morning against the forces of the Independent Free State of the Tyrant Helbida. The Tyrant's castle stood some miles up the valley. They didn't reach it until afternoon.

The Duke's forces halted in a rough semi-circle about the base of the castle and awaited orders. The castle was of black stone and seemed to grow out of the rugged valley wall. Flags flew from the battlements and occasionally a helmeted head could be seen peering over the edge.

There was a parley and one of the Good Duke's men rode into the castle through an opened postern. Some time later, the gate clanged open and the officer rode back, clutching the bleeding place in his face where his nose had been.

This decided the Duke. He waved his sword, the bugles blew loudly off key, and the men surged forward. They crushed around Grant, who clutched at the spear he had been issued and was pushed forward.

The air was filled with arrows and the roar and crash of battle. The first line of men carried wide shields and scaling ladders, which they placed against the sheer walls. Men were clambering up the ladders under a canopy of arrows from bowmen in the rear. Their fire was keeping the parapets fairly clear, but archers concealed behind the crenellations and fire slots poured down a withering rain of arrows at those on the ground.

Grant saw men dropping on all sides, but there were always more pressing from behind. Then he was in the comparative safety of the base of the wall, too close for the archers at the slots to see him. He got his hands on the rungs of a ladder and started to climb. At the next ladder he saw Aker Amen climbing rapidly. Grant climbed faster, wanting to get up level with Aker to give him a hail. The sight of the soldier's grin gave him a strange feeling of security in the midst of the surrounding carnage and death.

The man ahead fell off with a heavy rock bouncing from the top of his head, and Grant made an effort to catch him, then abandoned it and climbed rapidly through the clear ladder space ahead until he was two-thirds of the way up.

He turned, grinning, to shout to his Aker just in time to see an arrow pierce Aker's neck from side to side!

For an instant, the big soldier's hands held their grip on the ladder and Grant stared into the glazed sightless eyes. Then Aker was gone over the side of the ladder, gone forever, and there was another man there climbing up from below.

Something hot snapped in Grant's head. Without any dizzying transition or any feeling of sickness he was the berserker, cold with hate, and life became a simple matter of efficiently murdering the maximum number of the enemies of Aker Amen. He climbed.

Men were dying ahead of him, and then he was first man on the ladder. The top of the wall was ahead, and a bowman was peering down at him over a half-drawn bow. Grant drove his spear up into the man's eye socket and pulled it back with a savage thrill in his arms as the point crushed through flesh. The man fell past him like a harpooned fish. Grant mounted the top rung of the ladder and reached for the top of the wall just above him, and saw above that the incongruous form of a large stew kettle. For an instant his mind puzzled over the incongruity. What was a stew kettle doing in the middle of the battle? The thought faded as the fighting urge carried him up the wall.

But it was not a stew kettle he realized, as it tipped. The mouth turned more and more toward him and he felt a rush of warm air, a blast of radiated heat.

The giant pot tipped and the mouth was vertical. There was a sibilant rush and a silvery stream of molten lead gushed out. It seemed to hang over his head, then rush down, and he dropped his spear and ripped his throat in a terrible scream.

CHAPTER ELEVEN

"Look what you've done!"

"What?"

"That loose thread—just look where you stuffed it. It's all out of its own pattern and mixed up in this pattern over here."

"Well, put it back where it belongs. Don't bother me. Can't you see how busy I am repairing all the troubles you caused?"

"Troubles I caused? Why you..."

The angry voice was angrier now. The fumbling fingers caught at the misplaced thread, jerked it out and jammed it back into its own pattern. But not quite in the right place.

It all stopped. It stopped as suddenly as if a record had been broken, as suddenly as if a great hand, tiring of one station had spun a dial to another.

The battle shouts were gone, the pressure of the ladder rung was gone from Grant's curled fingers, and somewhere in the silence was a hollow distant booming, like the sound of surf heard down a tunnel. Burnt spots on his shoulder throbbed and hurt and a smell of singed hair and scorched leather was in his nostrils.

He could not see clearly, for the afterimage of what he had last seen still glared in his eyes. Like a curtain wherever he looked was the black silhouette of two men against the bright glare of the sky above, tilting their caldron of molten lead.

Grant blinked and the deadly image broke into a swirl of vague spots, through which walls and gray ceiling could be seen. Crouched, he lifted his free hand, still curled as if grasping the rung of a ladder that had gone, and brushed at the burning spots on his shoulder. Hot pebbles were dislodged from holes they had burned into cloth and leather and fell to clack on the floor—lead that had been cooled by burning into whatever it touched, lead that had been molten spatters from the great caldron. He remembered the wave of molten lead that had poured from the caldron down toward him. There had been no way to dodge. Why had only these few spatters touched him?

The thought of safety reached him at last, he straightened from his tense crouch. It had missed him, and he was alive, and he was grateful, but the understanding of it escaped him.

If the ladder had broken, part of the wall crumbled into an opening that he somehow managed to reach instead of falling or remaining on the ladder under that flood of fiery metal…he shuddered and turned his attention away from the thought to the problem of where he was.

If he were in the castle, he had fallen into a great opportunity, if he could only open one of the sallyports. A dim light filtered into the room through an open doorway, and a murmur of voices warned of danger on the other side. He pressed close to the wall and quickly glanced about him. Around the walls were boxes stacked on wheeled platforms. He was in some kind of small storeroom. The gray walls and ceiling were as smooth as the cloth of a tent and one corner of the room was crumpled down halfway to the floor, the ceiling and walls bent and wrinkled like a corner of a tent when an outside pole or guy rope is gone. Perhaps he had come in through an opening behind the cloth. It would be best to investigate, to have a way of escape when he needed one.

Grant took a silent stride toward it and prodded it with his sword, expecting to find it soft.

It was hard. He stretched up and gripped a projecting edge. It was very hard, strong and immovable under his hands, with a texture like cloth frozen in ice. Some gigantic hammer blow would have had to strike from the outside to have crumpled a corner of this tough material. The room was like a tin can that had been kicked by a giant.

How had he entered? Into whatever limbo of unconsciousness the time had gone, it could not have been more than five minutes since he was on the ladder. The attacking force outside could not have taken the castle. If he could get out the way he had come in, and bring back Aker and...

Memory came like a blow.

Aker was dead, an arrow driven through his throat. Grant put his hand to his eyes. He had seen warriors weep for friends and Aker was worthy of such tribute, but no tears came. Grant's early training in civilized inhibition held while the wave came and ebbed again. Dry-eyed and grim, he lowered his hand from before his eyes. The people clicking and murmuring in the next room were of the castle and the castle forces that had slain Aker. They were his enemies.

Grant shifted his sword from his left to his right, where it was as much a part of his arm as his hand itself, and stepped, silent and deadly, through the doorway. Fifteen men and women sat in a half circle, facing the wall. They were not armed, he decided against slaughter. They seemed young, and unmuscled, dressed in something like dark silk pajamas. The men were shaven and both sexes had their hair cut short and were as neat appearing as courtiers at the retinue of a king. A few of the women were topless. They sat in a crescent facing the curved wall tensely, concentrated on lights flashing in front of them, their hands busy over a shelf-like projection from the wall. The lights clicked and they murmured to each other occasionally in a sound like "Good!"

The wall made a complete circle. Near one end of the crescent was a monstrous gear wheel set into the wall with no apparent purpose, and close to Grant, directly behind their backs, was a door.

If they did not bother him, they were safe.

In silent strides, he reached the door and threw his weight against it. It was smooth-surfaced and cool, like metal, and it did not budge. There were no handles or bolts on the door. Grant stepped back and surveyed it, looking for the tell-tale smear of handprints that would show where to push to make it unlock, but the door was unmarred, a smooth, delicate green as if it were as fragile as egg shell.

He threw his weight against it, but it did not even tremble. It was metal, and a battering ram would not have dented it. It was strange to find metal thus used in a barbarian world where it was so scarce. A doubt was growing in his mind.

The crescent of people continued to work, unaware of him.

He turned to look beside the door for a hidden catch, but as he turned a lump of lead worked free from the leather of his corselet and landed on the floor with a skidding clatter.

Quietly, Grant turned to face the semicircle, lifting the point of his sword a little in their direction, warningly. Two or three faces turned and became astonished.

"Anyone shouts for help gets his throat slit to the backbone," he remarked to them, making sure his voice was clear enough to be heard by all.

The clicking ceased and a row of faces turned, identical smooth ovals with haggard eyes, as if they had not slept for many nights.

Startlingly, a voice from the wall spoke. "Do you see it too?"

"It's real," said one of the young women.

"Squad coming," said the voice from the wall. "Hold the line."

The fifteen turned back to the sloped shelf, poking buttons and twisting dials. Buttons clicked in and clicked out, dials turned and lights flashed in strange patterns in the picture frames before them. Grant was suddenly uncomfortable. The mechanisms smacked more of science than they did of this crude barbarian world. He shook the thought off—it must be magic of some kind. After all, this was an enchanter's castle.

The voice in the wall had said, *squad coming*, that he could understand. There ought to be another way out of the room. He had to make one of these people tell him. He slapped his sword against his calf and stepped forward, his voice sounding harsh and unreal in his ears.

"Where's the other way out? Speak up!"

They ignored him, and kept at their work at the control panels with concentrated intensity. They probably thought he was one of the castle warriors, drunk and straying out of bounds. Grant became irritated. He had only a few moments to escape and these were weaponless men, probably liege to the magician of the castle. He'd teach them to respect a fighting man.

He strode forward and put the edge of his sword along the center man's neck. "Answer," he bellowed. "Or I lop off a head."

They all jumped and alarm bells began ringing irritably all up and down the long panel. They corrected and silenced them with hasty jabs at the buttons.

The man with the sword at his neck gasped and pulled his head down between his shoulders as if he were a turtle, hoping to pull it entirely out of sight.

The two huge gears attracted Grant's eye; they were upright, side by side, and sunk into the wall, one so sunk that only its gear teeth showed where they meshed with the other. They were magnificent examples of simple sheer mechanics. The spaces between the huge gear teeth looked large enough for a man. It reminded him of something from the almost inconceivable time before he had been snatched away from his wedding…the compartments of a revolving door. The two gears were like intermeshed revolving doors.

Revolving door. That was it. He had a good guess where the second exit was. "Answer," he said to the sweating, trembling one with the sword at his neck.

A girl stood up and said indignantly. "Let him alone, you maniac!"

And a man farther along with the haggard eyes of all of them gave Grant a cold look that wished him to the lowest pits of hell and said, "Tell him where the second exit is, Chris."

"Oh, no!" She was dismayed, and gave a glance in the direction of the cogs. Her deserted control panel broke into tiny ringing bells and flashing lights and she hastily threw herself back onto the stool and tried to push enough buttons to quiet it.

The girl's glance had been worried and almost friendly, but it had told him more than she had meant. Grant had guessed right.

The double cog arrangement *was* a door. The tooth arrangement on one side kept anyone from coming in, for the entering side was filled by teeth of the second cog, but it did not keep anyone from going out. A squad would hesitate to follow him out into the arms of the besieging army.

He laughed aloud. "Thanks," he told the girl. Sheathing his sword, he sprang past her into a damp, salt-smelling compartment and threw his shoulder against its far side in a great heave. It began ponderously to move. In the room he was leaving there was the sound of a door slamming open, running footsteps and new voices. The squad had arrived.

Then the next gear tooth swung over and shut off the sound.

He pushed again. As the compartment revolved with him, an odd incomplete impression came to his mind; something in the control room had been familiar, *too* familiar. It was a thing that had been sitting on the girl's panel and it looked normal in a way that was oddly disturbing—a tankard of—of, what... Then with a shock he placed it.

The thing had been a cup, a normal plastic cup in a square modern design, with a spoon sticking out of the coffee in it. A thing from a world and a time that had seemed a million years in his past. There was no coffee in the barbarian world.

He was no longer in the castle. He was no longer in the same epoch or even the same world.

Where was he?

The strange door finished its swing. With the force of a fire hose, a wall of salt water smashed in, buffeted him against the back wall and filled the compartment before he had time to do more than draw a deep breath!

The revolving door had opened undersea.

CHAPTER TWELVE

With his sword clattering at his waist and tangling with his legs, with the weight of his weapons holding him to the bottom, and his quiver dragging in the water that was trying to stop him from moving, somehow Grant forced his way out of the compartment and fought his way up through the cold green unbreathable water to the surface.

The water grew lighter around him as he took the last few strokes, and then his head broke the surface and air and sky appeared around him.

After two deep breaths he sank again, the weight of his equipment pulling his head under. Exhausted, he had to swim back to the top. Ten feet away, a piece of driftwood bobbed in the swell and he swam to it, panting, needing most of his energy to stay up. It sank as he put his weight on it, but it held his head above the surface. It was a small, machine-cut beam with large bolts, and fitted well under one arm.

It was early morning, with the sun just risen over the horizon, turning the water in that direction to a sheet of white fire. The nearest land looked a good mile and a half away to the west, but there was a shiny thing that might have been a wrecked aircraft moving gently up and down in the swell only a quarter mile away. Some kind of planes or rockets were murmuring and buzzing high in the sky.

This was civilization. Perhaps the people undersea had set the coast guard to look for him. Grant thought wistfully of dry comfortable clothes and a good French dinner. Shifting his sword belt and bow to a more comfortable position, he began to swim, pushing the driftwood before him.

The sea heaved up and down, smooth and treacherous and beautiful, lapping over his face and filling his mouth every third breath as each wave passed him, moving toward the distant shore. He remembered with bitter humor the reaction of the people undersea to his demanding the "other way out." As an architect he had learned that a revolving door made a good pressure lock. The thick strength of the cogs should have warned him of the greatness of the pressure difference between inside and outside.

Perhaps the people in the dome had been scientists running some kind of a radar fire control test, but why had they worn uniforms that looked like pajamas? Had he returned to his own world?

Grant turned on his back to put his mouth higher and progressed at a considerably more rapid rate. A submerged on-the-back dog paddle was his best means of moving through the water. It would have had him expelled from his swimming class at Columbia, but it moved him in the direction he wanted to go and it held his mouth up so that he could breathe.

There were fleecy clouds high in the dark blue of the sky and somewhere above the clouds, perhaps in the stratosphere, unseen aircraft hummed in a multi-pitched whisper, crisscrossing and looping, leaving tangled threads of vapor trails.

One of the threads angled downward and stopped suddenly; there was a dot of black smoke high up in the clear blue where a ship had exploded.

Some indefinite time later, Grant ran into something hard with an unexpected thump on the top of his head. Turning over, he saw that he had reached the wrecked aircraft that was his goal.

There was a door to its interior, sprung half-open by a dent near the hinges, but it was too high to reach. The body of the aircraft was of some kind of white metal, like a standard alum alloy, but the design was different. The wingtip he had run into was raked back so far it was more like a fin on a rocket. Grant began to climb onto the fin, but the wet metal was slippery, and so streamlined there was nothing he could grip.

Taking advantage of the rise and fall of the sea, Grant slid up the fin, lying flat. Something in the added weight shifted the balance of the half-submerged craft. It rolled over a quarter turn and the fin swirled down and disappeared into the dark water and was gone, leaving him swimming again.

The turn of the wreck had brought the door opening down almost within teach.

He swam over to it, under the loom of the round sides, seeing his reflection in the wet metal as a face only, for the heavy weight of weapons and armor held him well below the surface. His legs were growing tired.

Below the doorway it looked impossibly out of reach, but he surged up with a sudden impatient energy and hooked one strong hand over the edge of the door, feeling the weight of everything he was wearing increase tremendously with the extra load of water they dragged along with them. With his hand over the edge of the opening, he rested, waiting to see if the wreck would roll again. The sea surged and fell with the man and the wreck, but the shattered aircraft did not roll.

Over the curve of the torpedo-shaped body, he could see holes three inches wide smashed through the metal. It was nothing that could happen to an aircraft by crashing into water. The plane had been shot down. Grant wondered who the fighting nations were.

As he hung there, he could feel the strain in his arms decreasing as the salt water drained from crannies of his armor and clothing.

He was light enough now to climb higher. With a quick heave, he pulled up enough to get an arm over the edge and brought his head up to look in over the sill. He saw a very large empty control cabin. Sunshine, reflected from water cast a cheerful wave-like glitter of running lights inside, over a large control board and a pilot's seat that oddly had two narrow backrests instead of one.

Behind the pilot's seat, on the floor in a great unaccountable heap, was a tangle of what looked like brown crisscrossed branches and logs with the rough bark still on.

Something was watching him.

The cheerful interior of the cabin was suddenly a nightmare, and Grant was frozen, fighting an impulse to slip back into the water. It was as if the cold eyes of cobras were watching him from behind that heap of branches. As if death moved close and waited.

He stared at the tangled branches, trying to see what was generating the fear he felt. And coldly, something glared back at him waiting. He could not see the stare, but he could feel it.

With every nerve in his body vibrating with warning, Grant cautiously swung one leg up and over the edge of the sill, and then completed his entrance in one move, rolling over once and onto his feet with his hand at his sword and ready.

The sword would not come out of its sheath. He yanked again but it was stuck.

The branches began to move, came up and out toward him, swiftly untangling as they came, as if a silent explosion in the center were pushing everything outward. For an instant Grant had the impression that someone was throwing these sticks and twigs at him, and then another nightmarish impression that they were *floating, slowing in midair.*

He stepped aside to avoid one and yanked again at his sword; his foot slipped in some oily green liquid that coated the deck, while—swollen by the water—the leather of the sheath gripped his sword and would not let it free.

In the next instant the heavy "branches" had spread out radially, almost completely filling the cabin like tapered spokes. Grant realized that their shape was changing, the tips curving in toward him. They were *flexing.*

Simultaneously he saw the eyes between the humped shoulders of the gigantic branched tentacles, between strange orifices that opened and closed meaninglessly. They were set on either side of the deep gash that opened into an interior of purple and green that oozed a slow seeping ichor. Red eyes glared hatred as the tentacles curved in toward him.

Between one thought and the next, Grant turned and dove back down into the welcoming sea.

He never reached it. Something hard and inflexible wrapped around his ankle and he banged against the ship's side. He looked over his shoulder and saw he was being dragged back by one of the branch-like tentacles. He forced down the rising panic and snatched an arrow out, fitting it to the bowstring. Grant drew back and aimed with the same motion, but a heave of the tentacle holding him brought him up to the door again and the arrow missed.

There was a sound that was not a voice, a wet, leathery gurgle. The grip on his ankle tightened with bone-crushing intensity. Grant tried to ignore the pain and, half upright now, sent another arrow after the first. This time it sank into one of the red eyes.

The tentacle gripped with a sudden spasm and then relaxed. He pulled the numb foot free and hurled himself backward out of the entrance. The bow was already slung across his shoulder when he hit the water.

He swam away, but not fast enough. A thin tentacle groped at him under the water and caught him around the waist. He clutched it away from his midriff and, sliding his dagger inside the loop, cut it away from his body.

As he splashed away this time it did not try to stop him. Perhaps it was dead. Grant had no desire to find out. He spotted his piece of driftwood nearby and swam towards it. Using it for support while he swam, he reached the surf by the time the sun was overhead.

The waves rolled him over and over a few times with rough humor before depositing him on the shore, shaking the arrows out of his quiver to roil in the surf.

CHAPTER THIRTEEN

For an hour or so Grant sat on the sand, patiently working his sword loose from the swollen sheath so he wouldn't rip the leather stitching. His armor was spread out on the sand around him, drying in the sun, and ever so often he would get up and patiently walk up and down along the line of surf, retrieving the few arrows the sea washed up.

When he finally separated sword and sheath, he set the soggy leather aside to dry and began to scour the rusting blade with sand.

Whatever the similarities of coffee and plastic cups, this world was not his world. Not with such monsters in it as the one aboard the plane. His sword and bow would probably be good friends.

While he was scouring, a thing like a jet plane hummed louder than the others, flying low and coming nearer, flying so low it seemed to be looking for something.

He remembered the monster in the wrecked airship on the sea and stopped moving and lay flat in the sand while the flying craft roared close by and past and the roar dwindled to distance again.

There was a possibility that the aircraft held friends, but his hunch persisted in visualizing a mass of waving tentacles covered with something like rough bark, sitting in a pilot's seat with two upright rods for a back rest—a back rest with room between the rods for tentacles to protrude, directing the jet while keen evil red eyes scanned for human shapes on the passing ground.

By the time the sun was beginning to slide down in the sky in the afternoon, thirst was making him restless, and an urge to find water for his dry throat was more than he could resist. Strapping his soggy armor and weapons back on, he started inland.

A brown fog seemed to hang over the land ahead as he walked, and the clean sea smell thickened to something subtly chemical and unpleasant.

Except for some low hills four or five miles away that showed traces of green, the land was as dead and desolate as the surface of the moon. The concrete road he walked on was broken and tilted; the ruins he passed looked as if they had been burned and shaken down by an earthquake and cratered by great holes.

A puddle of clean rainwater glistened in a hollow of the cracked cement, and Grant knelt to drink it, but the taste was strange and chemical, like the nauseous odor that hung in the air. Hastily he spat the water out and rose to his feet, swearingly thirsty.

For the first time he noticed the silence. Except for the hum and whisper of aircraft far away and out of sight in the sky, there was no sound, neither the distant hum of car motors and the blat of horns that would show the direction of a road still in use, nor even the distant barking of dogs which in all the ages and variations of humanity still marks the presence of a town.

Looking around, it seemed to him that the barren earth gave off the brown poisonous mist. Ahead was the wreck of larger buildings, with the brown fog wrapping itself around them.

The air he breathed was sickly with the chemical odor, until he could taste it in his mouth again even though he had spat out the rainwater. He walked on a little way, thinking seriously of turning back to the clean air of the seacoast.

Facing him on the road was the wreckage of a huge military tank. Its nose was dented in by a projectile that was still there, stuck half way in. It had probably been intended to burst on contact, but it was still there, unexploded, like a giant cigar in the mouth of a giant face.

Grant walked around it, looking in the gun slits at the variety of odd weapons, and then thought of water as suddenly as if he had heard the word. He turned back toward the sea, and then stopped.

Behind the tank had been its tracks, fresh tracks.

"Water," this time he heard the word clearly, though very faintly. His ear was so close to the side of the tank that he heard the feeble motion inside. The top hatch was open as if the occupants had escaped, but perhaps an automatic safety mechanism had done that, for a quick escape that was impossible because the occupant was wounded. Grant touched the side of the tank. It had heated all day under the sun, and the metal was searing.

The driver must be almost cooked by now. Shifting his sword belt behind him, Grant climbed to the top and called.

There was no answer except something that might have been a moan.

He climbed down inside.

Grant squeezed himself through the narrow passageway with his weapons clattering against the projecting edges of machinery. The air was intolerably hot, but it was comparatively clean air, without the poisonous miasmas of the outside fog.

At the end of the short passageway he found a tight little control room and a girl. The projectile that had hit the front of the tank had pushed the control panel almost to her chest and crushed in the control levers around her like a cage.

He knelt beside her and her eyes opened and she stared in wonder at the big man with the gentle expression and barbarian armor. She was brunette and pretty, in the same pajama style clothes as the undersea people.

"Anything I can do?" Grant asked, regretting now doubly that he had nothing to drink. One of her legs was literally pinned, pierced by a rod, and in the heat she must have been suffering thirst more agonizing than his.

She pointed past him, and he turned and saw a water container clipped to the wall.

For a few minutes thirst controlled him, but when he had partially stilled the fires within, he held it over her eager mouth. She drank until it was empty then collapsed back with a sigh. Sanity gradually returned to the girl's eyes and her cheeks began to flush.

Her eyes wandered over his strange clothing, the oddly long hair. "My name's Taftha Long. What's yours?"

"Grant O'Reilly."

"What are you doing in that strange costume, Grant O'Reilly?"

He thought for a minute and laughed grimly before replying. "Either I'm some kind of a time traveler or the victim of one of the most extended practical jokes ever played on a human being."

"What do you mean?" She looked bewildered.

It was inconceivable that anyone would believe the story he had to tell, so there was little point in telling it.

"It's a military secret." He leaned forward and kissed her lightly, and casually. "That's for being pretty. Now how about my getting you out of here? Would your leg bleed much if I pulled that rod out?"

She smiled, although growing pale again. "Could you...?"

For an answer he moved in close and began bending levers until he had space enough to get a good grip on the rod that pierced her thigh. It had missed the bone and gone straight into the muscle...it was a shapely thigh. He wrapped both hands around the rod.

"Brace yourself." He heaved and it gave under his hands and bent back and pulled from her leg, freeing her.

She shrieked briefly and sobbed until the pain dissipated. A moment later she was calm and self-disciplined again, staunching a flow of blood from the blue-black hole where the rod had been, pouring disinfectant in it and wrapping a bandage from a first-aid kit around it with quick military routine. Sweat stood out on her white face.

"What do you do now?" he asked, watching her. Her figure showed pleasingly, and she was clean and neat and efficient, unlike the women of the barbarian world. Yet compared to them, she was fragile and more like a little boy than a woman, with something cool and undeveloped in the way she moved. The stamp of a disciplined machine was on her.

"I'll finish delivering the formation cubes." She tried to stand up, wincing. He took an arm and helped her to her feet beside him in the narrow space. Her closeness stirred him, and the girl reminded him of Lucy. His hand closed tightly on the warm flesh of her arm, but she pulled free with an automatic gesture.

"I'm all stiff," she complained, "My foot is asleep." She stumbled toward the ladder and looked back to him gratefully. "I hope you have room for me in your tank."

He laughed. "I don't have a tank."

"But how did you get here? Nothing can live out there."

"I walked." He remembered the chemical smell in the air, the brown fog from the ground. "Why shouldn't anyone be able to live out there?"

She looked at him with the haggard, defeated eyes of the people underseas, and whispered. "Nothing can live out there. When the attack came, the gas…" She closed her eyes against a memory and leaned for awhile against the recoil mountings of the guns, with her breathing irregular and tears squeezing from under her eyelids.

Grant stood in his own private horror, seeing suddenly the vision of green Earth made dead and brown and decaying, with people and their cities and animals and birds alike vanished, the world a corpse. His voice was almost a whisper as he asked. "You're still fighting?"

She straightened defiantly. "We'll burn the atmosphere from the Earth before we let those things have it."

He thought with grim bitterness about the destroyed world her remark had implied. The human race was not doing so well in this version. He would not find his French restaurants except as burned ruins. For a moment, a fear came to mind that this was his own world, that these horrible changes had happened to it when he was gone, but he dismissed the idea. If there was one hope he had to cheer him, it was a hope that everything would change again as reasonlessly as the first time, and he would find himself in the safe friendly world he knew—an undestroyed world.

But this girl deserved better surroundings. If he had a hand on this girl the next time he went through to another world, could he take her with him? He liked the idea, but it seemed to be the farthest thing from the girl's mind.

All he could do was forget about it for awhile. He was in a wrecked tank in a destroyed world battling monsters. In a wrecked tank with a pretty girl, and she had an errand that he should help her with. But the tank interior was so narrow it was practically shoving her into his arms.

She looked at him with puzzlement. "I can't understand why you don't know these things. I thought all the survivors were in military bases underground."

"I wasn't." There was little possibility of explaining to her where he actually was while her version of Earth was being blasted and the human population she knew was dying. He considered trying to put it clearly into words, but his brain reeled. "You say they are still fighting?"

"We're holding them off."

Efficiently she was checking through the contents of an emergency kit she had pulled from some recess of the tank. "Here, fill this with water—there's a tap back there." She handed him a deflated balloon—like a water bottle. "We think that there aren't many left, and they probably have no more of the gas. If we can keep them from landing on Earth, the only materials they have to build more weapons are from the moon and asteroid belt. But if they find any more of the bases or underground factories, or find the control center for the automatic warheads, they could destroy it and get past the projectile screen."

Grant listened intently, filling the bottle at the water cooler while the plastic container inflated to the size and weight of a gallon bottle. He stood up and hitched it to his belt. What she was saying was hard to understand but it sounded like twentieth century warfare, and he struggled again with the uneasy feeling that this world might be his own world, horribly changed in his absence.

"You'll come along and enlist, won't you?" she asked appealingly.

The narrowness of the tank interior brought her against him again, and she was attractive. But her eyes were not aware of him—they were full of patriotic purpose.

He said, "I'll go along to make sure you don't get hurt."

She gave his primitive bow and arrows a puzzled glance but refrained from asking any questions. He had said it was a military secret and she was trained to respect that phrase. She slung a bag marked *Formation Cubes* across her shoulder and turned to the hatch.

Grant had to lift her up the ladder and out of the tank, for her injured leg was too stiff to bend and support her on the ladder. He enjoyed the contact; but once outside, she refused help and began limping along at a rapid rate.

They headed for the seacoast, away from the poisonous fogs of the land, and when they reached the sand, turned north. Grant took off his foot wrappings and strode along barefoot.

The hum of the aircraft overhead seemed nearer, and he could hear the faint popping of distant explosions. The thought came to him that this last stand of the human race could possibly end in defeat, and he wondered where they would hide if the tentacled invaders broke through those high defenses and landed on Earth as masters. The thought made him uneasy, and he glanced at the girl, to take reassurance from her confidence. But behind her tilted chin and determined limping stride there was the haggardness of the people underseas. The eyes, shadowed from looking towards a possible future that held a world devoid of the human race, showed the grimness of survivors who have learned that their species is not unconquerable—the responsibility of survivors who see no one else left alive to take responsibility. She limped on, not noticing his glance, intent on delivering the formation cubes.

"The fighting is coming closer to the ground," he said, striding beside her, with the water bottle gurgling faintly with every stride.

She glanced at the sky, paling. "Strategy," she said. "The Von Neuman players let them through unexpectedly every so often to break their formations, and then destroy more easily the ones that penetrate."

"Players?" He remembered the people at the control boards underseas and his fleeting impression that they were playing some sort of a game.

She explained. "Earth's best chess players, trained in the Von Neuman basic mathematics of competition and battle. They direct the remote-controlled weapons. The underground factories turn out remote-controlled proximity rockets, a steady stream of them, about ten a minute, and launch them, and the Von Neuman players send them up and keep them fighting in a solid defense shield in an unpredictable changing pattern that stops every attempt of the aliens to get through and land. The alien *things* have learned what's happening and have just one goal now, to find the control center of the weapons, the brain of all the rockets that attack them, and destroy it in one blow. But it's well-hidden, somewhere under the sea. We of my station don't even know where." She looked proud. *"They* won't ever find it. They grow weaker and fewer every day. Soon the rockets will have destroyed them."

Grant knew who the people undersea were now. They were the Players. He strode along silently for awhile, concealing a case of the shudders. He had been very close to killing the people underseas.

They passed a sandy bluff and the girl stopped, and studied the terrain inland, frowning in concentration, then pointed, her arm lovely and fragile.

"I think the station entrance is that way. I'm not sure; the tank was supposed to go in automatically on a subsonic guide note."

Grant helped her over the tumbled boulders to the broken sidewalks. They came to the wreckage of a small town and the subsonic vibrated against the soles of their feet like thunder in the distance, felt but not heard. Taftha stared from one building to another. Then suddenly broke into a limping run towards a half collapsed store.

"It's still there," she called. "The manual control! We can get in."

A gray metal box was built flush with the wall. She opened the lid and pushed buttons. There was a muffled rumbling and a tremendous heap of rubble stirred and humped slowly upward. A gap opened beneath the hump and widened and lifted until it was a tunnel mouth with a ramp big enough for a tank. Rock dust drifted away in a huge cloud as the rubble ceased to slide.

When the ground rumble ceased, they suddenly became aware that the sky sound had increased; the distant explosions above were not so distant and there was a thin, far-off whine that was increasing and nearing at terrifying speed, coming straight down. An alien ship was screaming toward them!

Taftha's face blanched under its coating of dust, and she tugged at his arm. "They must have been watching for it to open," she gasped starting for the opening. "*Run!*" she shrieked, as the whine became a roar.

Too late! The alien ship had been holed and riddled unmercifully on its way down, but it still operated. The forejets blasted fire, and the ship landed before the open portal like a wall dropping between them and refuge.

Grant only realized that Taftha had continued running when he saw her beside the alien ship, the formation cubes clutched tightly to her breasts, trying to run around the smoking bulk. But a port snapped open and a tree-like horror snaked across the ground and wrapped about her ankles. Taftha fell heavily, the formation cubes rolling ahead of her.

For one suspended instant of time Grant hesitated; this being was alive and deadly, not weakened like the one aboard the wrecked plane. A scream of pain from the girl decided him. When he leaped, it was towards the monster.

The speed of his attack saved him. Perhaps the dust, thick in the air, prevented it from noticing him. His sword whistled in a blurred arc and almost severed the tentacle holding Taftha. As it recoiled in pain, freeing her, his left arm caught about her waist. The inertia of his rush literally swept her from her feet and carried them well beyond the alien's reach. The mouth of the tunnel was before them. Grant veered to plunge into it.

Taftha's feet touched the ground and, with a desperate wriggle and a push, she squirmed out of his grip and ran back to the monster.

Grant looked on with amazement. Was the girl insane? No sooner had he rescued her then she turned back to the horror in the wrecked ship. Then he saw what she was doing, cursed and ran after her.

Those damned formation cubes! She had gone back for those doubly damned formation cubes. And the alien, with its tremendous other world vitality, was coming after her. She had the cubes, but as she turned—like a dream where there is no escape—the tentacles clutched her.

Grant stepped in again, sword swinging, but this time the alien was waiting. Grant sidestepped the first attack of twisting branched tentacles and hacked at those imprisoning Taftha. They released her and darted at him as she ran with the formation cubes, her eyes set ahead with only one purpose. Grant leaped away, too, and crashed his full length on the floor. Before he could turn and strike, the sword was dragged from his hand. Taftha disappeared through a side door of the tunnel.

The monster apparently felt the same revulsion towards him as he towards it. It held him with an almost human disgust.

The branching tentacles, some of them dripping a loathsome green from fresh wounds, seized and tore at him.

A tentacle tightened around his throat. Its twig-like projections broke through his skin and the larger tentacles were twisting his limbs from their sockets.

Through the red haze of pain he heard the voices. He knew he was dying and screamed aloud at the voices, but they did not hear.

"Grissel, look where you put that loose thread!"

"Look where she put it! I didn't go near it. It's all tangled up in the wrong places—you'd better cut it."

Grant, on the very borderline of death, passed over. The voices were fading.

"You can't cut it. The whole design will ravel. I'll weave it into these loose parts here, and later we will have to use it in the design there."

"I don't think it should go there, it wouldn't fit in at all..."

The voices died at the moment Grant lived. The tentacles vanished and he was rolling down a hillside. He thumped against a boulder and sat up, rubbing the snow from his face.

Snow! Then he must be back in the world of the barbarians. It wasn't the best place to be, but at least he knew how to make his way around there. Rubbing his bruised limbs, he searched in the drifts for his sword. There was no trace of it around the spot where he had landed. It must still be with the alien from space. He shuddered a little at the memory. As if in echo of his thoughts, a soul-piercing scream came from a grove nearby. The hackles rose on his neck and he jumped to put his back to the rock as he tore out his dagger.

His elbows were braced against the rock, the dagger straight out before him. If it was a Berl-Cat he didn't stand much of a chance, but anything else would have a fight on its hands—or paws.

There was the thumping of many feet, branches cracked and broke as the screaming came nearer. Grant wiped some, of the blood from his slippery hands and braced himself for the attack.

Around the rock they came, twenty of them. Their multicolored clothes snapped in the wind as they ran. They stopped suddenly when they saw Grant's ragged and bloody figure. Then, screaming now with terror, they turned and fled.

Grant lowered his dagger. Just children playing in the snow. Children in coats and leggings waving toy pistols.

Toy pistols!

He looked up at the gray cliffs, just visible through the winter haze. They seemed to move in his vision, as he looked with his mind as well as his eyes, and he saw that they weren't cliffs at all, but giant buildings. He looked at a scenic bridge in the hollow and remembered it—and the buildings and the children.

He was in Central Park.

Home again, back in his own world! The strength drained from his legs and he sat heavily on a boulder. Home again, back in the world he never expected to see.

It was home, the buildings, the children, the familiar clothes they wore. A cold finger of doubt touched him suddenly. Did kids wear those funny beanies with propellers on the top? He couldn't remember. Was he home—or almost home? Or perhaps a few years early—or late?

The thoughts were disquieting. So was the memory of those voices he had heard. They had something to do with his going from world to world. What *had* they said? Something about going *here* and *later* there. Was *here* home or was *there*?

There was a crackling of branches again, in the woods. A blue-coated policeman was puffing as he pulled himself up the slope.

Grant could detect nothing wrong in his uniform.

As suddenly as they had come, the fears were swept away. Grant climbed to his feet and smiled at the world. He had had enough of being afraid. He would get along here, whether it was his own world or not. It didn't make that much difference anymore. It didn't even matter what his mother would say about his ragged clothes, if this were home.

He slid his dagger back into the sheath and, smiling to himself, went down to meet the worried policeman.

THE END

If you've enjoyed this book, you will not want to miss these terrific titles...

If you've enjoyed this book, you will not want to miss these terrific titles...

ARMCHAIR SCI-FI & HORROR DOUBLE NOVELS, $12.95 each

D-61   **THE MAN WHO STOPPED AT NOTHING** by Paul W. Fairman
          TEN FROM INFINITY by Ivar Jorgensen

D-62   **WORLDS WITHIN** by Rog Phillips
          THE SLAVE by C.M. Kornbluth

D-63   **SECRET OF THE BLACK PLANET** by Milton Lesser
          THE OUTCASTS OF SOLAR III by Emmett McDowell

D-64   **WEB OF THE WORLDS** by Harry Harrison and Katherine MacLean
          RULE GOLDEN by Damon Knight

D-65   **TEN TO THE STARS** by Raymond Z. Gallun
          THE CONQUERORS by David H. Keller, M. D.

D-66   **THE HORDE FROM INFINITY** by Dwight V. Swain
          THE DAY THE EARTH FROZE by Gerald Hatch

D-67   **THE WAR OF THE WORLDS** by H. G. Wells
          THE TIME MACHINE by H. G. Wells

D-68   **STARCOMBERS** by Edmond Hamilton
          THE YEAR WHEN STARDUST FELL by Raymond F. Jones

D-69   **HOCUS-POCUS UNIVERSE** by Jack Williamson
          QUEEN OF THE PANTHER WORLD by Berkeley Livingston

D-70   **BATTERING RAMS OF SPACE** by Don Wilcox
          DOOMSDAY WING by George H. Smith

ARMCHAIR SCIENCE FICTION & FANTASY CLASSICS, $12.95 each

C-19   **EMPIRE OF JEGGA**
          by David V. Reed

C-20   **THE TOMORROW PEOPLE**
          by Judith Merril

C-21   **THE MAN FROM YESTERDAY**
          by Howard Browne as by Lee Francis

C-22   **THE TIME TRADERS**
          by Andre Norton

C-23   **ISLANDS OF SPACE**
          by John W. Campbell

C-24   **THE GALAXY PRIMES**
          by E. E. "Doc" Smith

BE DONE BY, AS YOU DO TO OTHERS...

A man in Des Moines kicked his wife when her back was turned. She was taken to the hospital, suffering from a broken coccyx. Amazingly, so was he. In Kansas City, a youth armed with a .22 killed a schoolmate with one shot, then dropped dead himself. A mystery swept over the slaughterhouses of Chicago as workers began collapsing inexplicably. As one victim put it: "It felt just like I was hit in the head." In St. Louis, a policeman shot down a fleeing bank robber, then collapsed. The bank robber died; the policeman's condition was listed as critical.

With a nifty little twist of humanity's golden rule, "Do Unto Others," Damon Knight once again brings another powerful tale to the table. Knight was a prolific science fiction writer, editor, critic and fan. His forte was short stories and he is still widely acknowledged as one of the true masters of the genre. He won the esteemed Hugo award and was the founder of the Science Fiction and Fantasy Writers of America.

CAST OF CHARACTERS

ROBERT DAHL
His suspicions led him to the story of the decade—the story of a life and death struggle that encompassed all of Earth's species!

AZA-KRA
This alien had no trouble in justifying the extinction of carnivores—from his point of view, they were all better off dead.

CAPTAIN RITCHY-LOO
Assigned as an escort to Dahl, he needed to keep things under control and under wrap—not what you'd call an easy task!

GEORGE WHEELWRIGHT
Everyone's got a talent for something. George's happened to be in passport forgery. But what could he do for a six-eyed alien?

MAJOR GENERAL PARST
A big, bald smooth operator, he had no intention of letting anyone in, or anything out of his military compound…alive.

CARLTON FRISBEE
A career man all the way… he wouldn't let a newspaper man's tale foul up the works. His motto: write the story my way, or die.

RULE
GOLDEN

By
DAMON KNIGHT

ARMCHAIR FICTION
PO Box 4369, Medford, Oregon 97504

For more information about Armchair Books and products, visit our website at...

www.armchairfiction.com

Or email us at...

armchairfiction@yahoo.com

CHAPTER ONE

A man in Des Moines kicked his wife when her back was turned. She was taken to the hospital, suffering from a broken coccyx.

So was he.

In Kansas City, Kansas, a youth armed with a .22 killed a schoolmate with one shot through the chest, and instantly dropped dead of heart failure.

In Decatur two middleweights named Packy Morris and Leo Oshinsky simultaneously knocked each other out.

In St. Louis, a policeman shot down a fleeing bank robber and collapsed. The bank robber died; the policeman's condition was described as critical.

I read those items in the afternoon editions of the Washington papers, and although I noted the pattern, I wasn't much impressed. Every newspaperman knows that runs of coincidence are a dime a dozen; *everything* happens that way—plane crashes, hotel fires, suicide pacts, people running amok with rifles, people giving away all their money; name it and I can show you an epidemic of it in the files.

What I was actually looking for were stories originating in two places: my hometown and Chillicothe, Missouri. Stories with those datelines had been carefully cut out of the papers before I got them, so, for lack of anything better, I read everything datelined near either place. And that was how I happened to catch the Des Moines, Kansas City, Decatur and St. Louis items—all of those places will fit into a two-hundred-mile circle drawn with Chillicothe as its center.

I had asked for, but hadn't got, a copy of my own paper. That made it a little tough, because I had to sit there in a Washington hotel room at night—and if you know a lonelier place and time, tell me—and wonder if they had really shut us down.

I knew it was unlikely. I knew things hadn't got that bad in America yet, by a long way. I knew they *wanted* me to sit there and worry about it, but I couldn't help it.

Ever since *La Prensa,* every newspaper publisher on this Continent has felt a cold wind blowing down his back.

That's foolishness, I told myself. Not to wave the flag too much or anything, but the free speech tradition in this country is too strong; we haven't forgotten Peter Zenger.

And then it occurred to me that a lot of editors must have felt the same way, just before their papers were suppressed on the orders of an American President named Abraham Lincoln.

So I took one more turn around the room and got back into bed, and although I had already read all the papers from bannerlines to box scores, I started leafing through them again, just to make a little noise. Nothing to do.

I had asked for a book, and hadn't got it. That made sense, too; there was nothing to do in that room, nothing to distract me, nothing to read except newspapers—and how could I look at a newspaper without thinking of the *Herald-Star?*

My father founded the *Herald-Star*—the *Herald* part, that is, the *Star* came later—ten years before I was born. I inherited it from him, but I want to add that I'm not one of those publishers by right of primogeniture whose only function consists in supplying sophomoric by-lined copy for the front page; I started on the paper as a copy boy and I can still handle any job in a city room.

It was a good newspaper. It wasn't the biggest paper in the Middle West, or the fastest growing, or the loudest; but we'd had two Pulitzer prizes in the last fifteen years, we kept our political bias on the editorial page and up to now we had never knuckled under to anybody.

But this was the first time we had picked a fight with the U. S. Department of Defense.

Ten miles outside Chillicothe, Missouri, the Department had a little hundred-acre installation with three laboratory buildings, a small airfield, living quarters for a staff of two hundred and a one-story barracks. It was closed down in 1958 when the Phoenix-bomb program was officially abandoned.

Two years and ten months later, it was opened up again. A new and much bigger barracks went up in place of the old one; a two-company garrison moved in. Who else or what else went into the area, nobody knew for certain; but rumors came out.

We checked the rumors. We found confirmation. We published it, and we followed it up. Within a week we had a full-sized crusade started; we were asking for a congressional investigation, and it looked as if we might get it.

Then the President invited me and the publishers of twenty-odd other anti-administration dailies to Washington. Each of us got a personal interview with The Man; the Secretary of Defense was also present, to evade questions.

They asked me, as a personal favor and in the interests of national security, to kill the Chillicothe series.

After asking a few questions, to which I got the answers I expected, I politely declined.

And here I was.

The door opened. The guard outside looked in, saw me on the bed, and stepped back out of sight. Another man walked in: stocky build, straight black hair turning gray; about fifty. Confident eyes behind rimless bifocals.

"Mr. Dahl. My name is Carlton Frisbee."

"I've seen your picture," I told him. Frisbee was the Under Secretary of Defense, a career man, very able; he was said to be the brains of the Department.

He sat down facing me. He didn't ask permission, and he didn't offer to shake hands, which was intelligent of him.

"How do you feel about it now?" he asked.

"Just the same."

He nodded. After a moment he said, "I'm going to try to explain our position to you, Mr. Dahl."

I grinned at him. "The word you're groping for is 'awkward.'"

"No. It's true that we can't let you go in your present state of mind, but we can keep you.

If necessary, you will be killed, Mr. Dahl. That's how important Chillicothe is."

"Nothing," I said, "is that important."

He cocked his head at me. "If you and your family lived in a community surrounded by hostile savages, who were kept at bay only because you had rifles—and if someone proposed to give them rifles—well?"

"Look," I said, "let's get down to cases. You claim that a new weapon is being developed at Chillicothe, is that right? It's something revolutionary, and if the Russians got it first we would be sunk, and so on. In other words, the Manhattan Project all over again."

"Right."

"Okay. Then why has Chillicothe got twice the military guard it had when it was an atomic research center, and a third of the civilian staff?"

He started to speak.

"Wait a minute, let me finish. Why, of the fifty-one scientists we have been able to trace to Chillicothe, are seventeen linguists and philologists, three organic chemists, five physiologists, *twenty-six psychologists, and not one single physicist?*"

"In the first place—were you about to say something?"

"All right, go ahead."

"You know I can't answer those questions factually. Mr. Dahl, but speaking conjecturally, can't you conceive of a psychological weapon?"

"You can't answer them at all. My third question is, why have you got a wall around that place—not just a stockade, a wall, with guard towers on it? Never mind speaking conjecturally. Now I'll answer your question. Yes, I can conceive of psychological experimentation that you might call weapons research. I can think of several possibilities, and there isn't a damn one of them that wouldn't have to be used on American citizens before you could get anywhere near the Russians with it."

His eyes were steady behind the bright lenses. He didn't say, "We seem to have reached a deadlock," or "Evidently it would be useless to discuss this any further"; he simply changed the subject.

"There are two things we can do with you, Mr. Dahl; the choice will be up to you. First, we can indict you for treason and transfer you to a Federal prison to await trial. Under the revised Alien and Sedition Act, we can hold you incommunicado for at least twelve months, and, of course, no bail will be set. I feel bound to point out to you that in this case, it would be impossible to let you come to trial until after the danger of breaching security at Chillicothe is past. If necessary, as I told you, you would die in prison.

"Second, we can admit you to Chillicothe itself as a press representative. We would, in this case, allow you full access to all non-technical information about the Chillicothe project as it develops, with permission to publish as soon as security is lifted. You would be confined to the project until that time, and, I can't offer you any estimate of how long it might be. In return, you would be asked to write letters plausibly explaining your absence to your staff and to close friends and relatives, and—providing that you find Chillicothe to be what we say it is and not what you suspect—to work out a series of stories for your newspaper which will divert attention from the project."

He seemed to be finished. I said, "Frisbee, I hate to tell you this, but you're overlooking, a point. Let's just suppose for a minute that Chillicothe is what I think it is. How do I know that once I got inside I might not somehow or other find myself writing that kind of copy whether I felt like it or not?"

He nodded. "What guarantees would you consider sufficient?"

I thought about that. It was a nice point. I was angry enough, and scared enough, to feel like pasting Frisbee a good one and then seeing how far I could get; but one thing I couldn't figure out, and that was why, if Frisbee wasn't at least partly on the level, he should be here at all.

If they wanted me in Chillicothe, they could drag me there.

After awhile I said, "Let me call my managing editor and tell him where I'm going. Let me tell him that I'll call him again—*on a video circuit*—within three days after I get there, when I've had time to inspect the whole area. And that if I don't call, or if I look funny or sound funny, he can start worrying."

He nodded again. "Fair enough." He stood up. "I won't ask you to shake hands with me now, Mr. Dahl; later on I hope you will." He turned and walked to the door, unhurried, calm, imperturbable, the way he had come in.

Six hours later I was on a westbound plane.

That was the first day.

The second day, an inexplicable epidemic broke out in the slaughterhouses of Chicago and surrounding areas. The symptoms were a sudden collapse followed by nausea, incontinence, anemia, shock, and in some eases, severe pain in the occipital and cervical regions. Or: as one victim, an A.F. of L. knacker with twenty-five years' experience in the nation's abattoirs, succinctly put it: "It felt just like I was hit in the head."

Local and Federal health authorities immediately closed down the affected slaughterhouses, impounded or banned the sale of all supplies of fresh meat in the area, and launched a sweeping investigation. Retail food stores sold out their stocks of canned, frozen and processed meats early in the day; seafood markets reported their largest volume of sales in two decades. Eggs and cheese were in short supply.

Fifty-seven guards, assistant wardens and other minor officials of the Federal penitentiary at Leavenworth, Kansas, submitted a group resignation to Warden Hermann R. Longo. Their explanation of the move was that all had experienced a religious conversion, and that assisting in the forcible confinement of other human beings was inconsonant with their new beliefs.

Near Louisville, Kentucky, neighbors attracted by cries for help found a forty-year-old woman and her twelve-year-old daughter both severely burned. The woman, whose clothing was not even scorched although her upper body was covered with first and second degree burns, admitted pushing the child into a bonfire, but in her hysterical condition was unable to give a rational account of her own injuries.

There was also a follow-up on the Des Moines story about the man who kicked his wife. Remember that I didn't say he had a broken coccyx; I said he was suffering from one. A few hours after he was admitted to the hospital he stopped doing so, and he was released into police custody when X-rays showed no fracture.

Straws in the wind.

At five-thirty that morning, I was waking up my managing editor, Eli Freeman, with a monitored long-distance call—one of Frisbee's bright young men waiting to cut me off if I said anything I shouldn't. The temptation was strong, just the same, but I didn't.

From six to eight-thirty I was on a plane with three taciturn guards. I spent most of the time going over the last thirty years of my life, and wondering how many people would remember me two days after they wrapped my obituary around their garbage.

We landed at the airfield about a mile from the Project proper, and after one of my hitherto silent friends had finished a twenty-minute phone call, a limousine took us over to a long, temporary-looking frame building just outside the wall. It took me only until noon to get out again; I had been fingerprinted, photographed, stripped, examined, X-rayed, urine analyzed, blood-tested, showered, disinfected, and given a set of pinks to wear until my own clothes had been cleaned and fumigated. I also got a numbered badge which I was instructed to wear on the left chest at all times, and an identity card to keep in my wallet when I got my wallet back.

Then they let me through the gate, and I saw Chillicothe.

I was in a short cul-de-sac formed by the gate and two walls of masonry, blank except for firing slits. Facing away from the gate I could see one of the three laboratory buildings a good half-mile away. Between me and it was a geometrical forest of poles with down-pointing reflectors on their crossbars. Floodlights.

I didn't like that. What I saw a few minutes later I liked even less. I was bouncing across the flat in a jeep driven by a stocky, moon-faced corporal; we passed the first building, and I saw the second.

There was a ring of low pillboxes around it. And their guns pointed *inward*, toward the building.

Major General Parst was a big, bald man in his fifties, whose figure would have been more military if the Prussian corset had not gone out of fashion. I took him for a Pentagon soldier; he had the Pentagon smoothness of manner, but there seemed to be a good deal more under it than the usual well oiled vacancy. He was also, I judged, a very worried man.

"There's just one thing I'd like to make clear to you at the beginning, Mr. Dahl. I'm not a grudge-holding man, and I hope you're not either, because there's a good chance that you and I will be seeing a lot of each other during the next three or four years. But I thought it might make it a little easier for you to know that you're not the only one with a grievance. You see this isn't an easy job, it never has been. I'm just stating the fact: it's been considerably harder since your newspaper took an interest in us." He spread his hands and smiled wryly.

"Just what is your job, General?"

"You mean, what is Chillicothe," He snorted. "I'm not going to waste my breath telling you."

My expression must have changed.

"Don't misunderstand me—I mean that if I told you, you wouldn't believe me. I didn't, myself. I'm going to have to show you." He stood up, looking at his wristwatch. "I have a little more than an hour. That's more than enough for the demonstration, but you're going to have a lot of questions afterward. We'd better start."

He thumbed his intercom, "I'll be in Section One for the next fifteen minutes."

When we were in the corridor outside he said, "Tell me something, Mr. Dahl: I suppose it occurred to you that if you were right in your suspicions of Chillicothe, you might be running a certain personal risk in coming here, in spite of any precautions you might take?"

"I considered the possibility. I haven't seen anything to rule it out yet."

"And still, I gather that you chose this alternative almost without hesitation. Why was that, if you don't mind telling me?"

It was a fair question. There's nothing very attractive about a Federal prison, but at least they don't saw your skull open there, or turn your mind inside out with drugs. I said, "Call it curiosity."

He nodded. "Yes. A very potent force, Mr. Dahl. More mountains have been moved by it than by faith."

We passed a guard with a T44, then a second, and a third. Finally Parst stopped at the first of three metal doors. There was a small pane of thick glass set into it at eye-level, and what looked like a microphone grill under that. Parst spoke into the grill: "Open up Three, sergeant."

"Yes, sir."

I followed Parst to the second door. It slid open as we reached it and we walked into a large, empty room. The door closed behind us with a thud and a solid *click*. Both sounds rattled back startlingly; the room was solid metal, I realized— floor, walls and ceiling.

In the opposite wall was another heavy door. To my left was a huge metal hemisphere, painted the same gray as the walls, with a machine-gun's snout projecting through a horizontal slit in a deadly and impressive manner.

Echoes blurred the General's voice: "This is Section One. We're rather proud of it. The only entrance to the central room is here, but each of the three others that adjoin it is covered from a gun-turret like that one. The gun rooms are accessible only from the corridors outside."

He motioned me over to the other door. "This door is double," he said. "It's going to be an airlock eventually, we hope. All right, sergeant!"

The door slid back, exposing another one a yard farther in; like the others, it had a thick inset panel of glass.

Parst stepped in and waited for me. "Get ready for a shock," he said.

I loosened the muscles in my back and shoulders; my wind isn't what it used to be, but I can still hit. *Get ready for one yourself,* I thought, *if this is what I think it is.*

I walked into the tiny room, and heard the door thump behind me. Parst motioned to the glass pane.

I saw a room the size of the one behind me. There was a washbasin in it, and a toilet, and what looked like a hammock slung across one corner, and a wooden table with papers and a couple of pencils or crayons on it.

And against the far wall, propped upright on an ordinary lunch-counter stool, was something I couldn't recognize at all. I saw it and I didn't see it. If I had looked away then, I couldn't possibly have told anyone what it looked like.

Then it stirred slightly, and I realized that it was alive.

I saw that it had eyes.

I saw that it had arms.

I saw that it had legs.

Very gradually the rest of it came into focus. The top about four feet off the floor, a small truncated cone about the size and shape of one of those cones of string that some merchants keep to tie packages. Under that came the eyes, three of them. They were round and oyster-gray, with round black pupils, and they faced in different directions. They were set into a flattened bulb of flesh that just fitted under the base of the cone; there was no nose, no ears, no mouth, and no room on the flesh for any.

The cone was black; the rest of the thing was a very dark, shiny blue-gray.

The head, if that is the word, was supported by a thin neck from which a sparse growth of fuzzy spines curved down and outward, like a botched attempt at feathers. The neck thickened gradually until it became the torso. The torso was shaped something like a bottle gourd, except that the upper lobe was almost as large as the lower. The upper lobe expanded and contracted evenly, all around, as the thing breathed.

Between each arm and the next, the torso curved inward to form a deep vertical gash.

There were three arms and three legs, spaced evenly around the body so that you couldn't tell front from back. The arms sprouted just below the top of the torso, the legs from its base. The legs were bent only slightly to reach the floor; each hand, with five slender, shapeless fingers, rested on the opposite number thigh. The feet were a little like a chicken's.

I turned away and saw Parst; I had forgotten he was there, and where I was, and who I was, I don't recall planning to say anything, but I heard my own voice, faint and hoarse:

"Did you *make* that?"

CHAPTER TWO

"Stop it!" he said sharply.

I was trembling. I had fallen into a crouch without realizing it, weight on my toes, fists clenched.

I straightened up slowly and put my hands into my pockets. "Sorry."

The speaker rasped.

"Is everything all right, sir?"

"Yes, sergeant," said Parst. "We're coming out." He turned as the door opened, and I followed him, feeling all churned up inside.

Halfway down the corridor I stopped. Parst turned and looked at me.

"Ithaca," I said.

Three months back there had been a Monster-from-Mars scare in and around Ithaca, New York; several hundred people had seen, or claimed to have seen, a white wingless aircraft hovering over various out-of-the-way places; and over thirty, including one very respectable Cornell professor, had caught sight of something that wasn't a man in the woods around Cayuga Lake. None of these people had got close enough for a good look, but nearly all of them agreed on one point—the thing walked erect, but had too many arms and legs...

"Yes," said Parst. "That's right. But let's talk about it in my office, Mr. Dahl."

I followed him back there. As, soon as the door was shut I said, "Where did it come from? Are there any more of them? What about the ship?"

He offered me a cigarette. I took it and sat down, hitting the chair by luck.

"Those are just three of the questions we can't answer," he said. "He claims that his home world revolves around a sun in our constellation of Aquarius; he says that it isn't visible from Earth. He also—"

I said, "He talks—? You've taught him to speak English?" For some reason that was hard to accept; then I remembered the linguists.

"Yes. Quite well, considering that he doesn't have vocal cords like ours. He uses a tympanum under each of those vertical openings in his body—those are his mouths. His name is Aza-Kra, by the way. I was going to say that he also claims to have come here alone. As for the ship, he says it's hidden, but he won't tell us where. We've been searching that area, particularly the hills near Cayuga and the lake itself, but we haven't turned it up yet. It's been suggested that he may have launched it under remote control and put it into an orbit somewhere outside the atmosphere. The Lunar Observatory is watching for it, and so are the orbital stations, but I'm inclined to think that's a dead end. In any case, that's not my responsibility. He had some gadgets in his possession when he was captured, but even those are being studied elsewhere. Chillicothe is what you saw a few minutes ago, and that's all it is. God knows it's enough."

His intercom buzzed. "Yes."

"Dr. Meshevski would like to talk to you about the technical vocabularies, sir."

"Ask him to hold it until the conference if he possibly can."

"Yes sir."

"Two more questions we can't answer," Parst said, "are what his civilization is like and what he came here to do. I'll tell you what he says. The planet he comes from belongs to a galactic union of highly advanced, peace-loving races. He came here to help us prepare ourselves for membership in that union."

I was trying hard to keep up, but it wasn't easy. After a moment I said, "Suppose it's true?"

He gave me the cold eye.

"All right, suppose it's true." For the first time, his voice was impatient. "Then suppose the opposite. Think about it for a minute."

I saw where he was leading me, but I tried to circle around to it from another direction; I wanted to reason it out for myself. I couldn't make the grade; I had to fall back on analogies, which are a kind of thinking I distrust.

You were a cannibal islander, and a missionary came along. He meant well, but you thought he wanted to steal your yam-fields and your wives, so you chopped him up and ate him for dinner.

Or:

You were a West Indian, and Columbus came along. You treated him as a guest, but he made a slave of you, worked you till you dropped, and finally wiped out your whole nation, to the last woman and child.

I said, "Awhile ago you mentioned three or four years as the possible term of the Project. Did you—?"

"That wasn't meant to be taken literally," he said. "It may take a lifetime." He was staring at his desktop.

"In other words, if nothing stops you, you're going to go right on just this way, sitting on this thing. Until What's-his-name dies, or his friends show up with an army, or something else blows it wide open."

"*That's* right."

"Well, damn it, don't you see that's the one thing you can't do? Either way you guess it that won't work. If he's friendly—"

Parst lifted a pencil in his hand and slapped it palm-down against the desktop. His mouth was tight. "It's *necessary,*" he said.

After a silent moment he straightened in his chair and spread the fingers of his right hand at me. "One," he said, touching the thumb: "weapons. Leaving everything else aside, if we can get one strategically superior weapon out of him, or the theory that will enable us to build one, then we've *got* to do it and we've *got* to do it in secret."

The index finger. "Two: the spaceship." Middle finger. "Three: the civilization he comes from. If they're planning to attack us we've got to find that out, and when, and how, and what we can do about it." Ring finger. "Four: Aza-Kra himself. If we don't hold him in secret we can't hold him at all, and how do we know what he might do if we let him go? There isn't a single possibility we can rule out. Not one."

He put the hand flat on the desk. "Five, six, seven, eight, nine, ten, infinity. Biology, psychology, sociology, ecology, chemistry, physics, right down the line. Every science. In any one of them we might find something that would mean the difference between life and death for this country or this whole planet."

He stared at me for a moment, his face set. "You don't have to remind me of the other possibilities, Dahl. I know what they are; I've been on this project for thirteen weeks. I've also heard of the Golden Rule, and the Ten Commandments, and the Constitution of the United States. But this is *the survival of the human race* we're talking about."

I opened my mouth to say "That's just the point," or something equally stale, but I shut it again; I saw it was no good. I had one argument—that if this alien ambassador was what he claimed to be, then the whole world had to know about it; any nation that tried to suppress that knowledge, or dictate the whole planet's future, was committing a crime against humanity. That, on the other hand, if he was an advance agent for an invasion fleet, the same thing was true only a great deal more so.

Beyond that I had nothing but instinctive moral conviction; and Parst had that on his side too; so did Frisbee and the President and all the rest. Being who and what they were, they had to believe as they did. Maybe they were right.

Half an hour later, the last thought I had before my head hit the pillow was, *Suppose there isn't any Aza-Kra? Suppose that thing was a fake, a mechanical dummy?*

But I knew better, and I slept soundly.

That was the second day. On the third day, the front pages of the more excitable newspapers were top-heavy with forty-eight-point headlines. There were two Chicago stories. The first, in the early afternoon editions, announced that every epidemic victim had made a complete recovery, that health department experts had been unable to isolate any disease-causing agent in the stock awaiting slaughter, and that although several cases not involving stockyard employees had been reported, not one had been traced to consumption of infected meat. A Chicago epidemiologist was quoted as saying, "It could have been just a gigantic coincidence."

The later story was a lulu. Although, the slaughterhouses had not been officially reopened or the ban on fresh-meat sales rescinded, health officials allowed seventy of the previous day's victims to return to work as an experiment. Within half an hour every one of them was back in the hospital, suffering from a second identical attack.

Oddly enough—at first glance—sales of fresh meat in areas outside the ban dropped slightly in the early part of the day ("They *say* it's all right, but you won't catch me taking a chance"), but rose sharply in the evening ("I'd better stock up before there's a run on the butcher shops").

Warden Longo, in an unprecedented move, added his resignation to those of the fifty-seven "conscience" employees of Leavenworth. Well-known as an advocate of prison reform, Longo explained that his subordinates' example had convinced him that only so dramatic a gesture could focus the American public's attention upon the injustice and inhumanity of the present system.

He was joined by two hundred and three of the Federal institution's remaining employees, bringing the total to more than eighty per cent of Leavenworth's permanent staff.

The movement was spreading. In Terre Haute, Indiana, eighty employees of the Federal penitentiary were reported to have resigned. Similar reports came from the State prisons of Iowa, Missouri, Illinois and Indiana, and from city and county correctional institutions from Kansas City to Cincinnati.

The war in Indo-China was crowded back among the stock market reports. Even the official announcements that the first Mars rocket was nearing completion in its sublunar orbit—front-page news at any normal time—got an inconspicuous paragraph in some papers and were dropped entirely by others.

But I found an item in a St. Louis paper about the policeman who had collapsed after shooting a criminal. He was dead.

I woke up a little before dawn that morning, having had a solid fifteen hours' sleep, I found the cafeteria and hung around until it opened. That was where Captain Ritchy-loo tracked me down.

He came in as I was finishing my second order of ham and eggs, a big, blond, swimming-star type full of confidence and good cheer. "You must be Mr. Dahl. My name is Ritchy-loo."

I let him pump my hand and watched him sit down. "How do you spell it?" I asked him.

He grinned happily. "It is a tough one, isn't it? French. R, i, c, h, e, l, i, e, u."

Richelieu. Ritchy-loo.

I said, "What can I do for you, Captain?"

"Ah, it's what I can do for *you,* Mr. Dahl. You're a VIP around here, you know. You're getting the triple-A guided tour, and I'm your guide."

I *hate* people who are cheerful in the morning.

We went out into the pale glitter of early-morning sunshine on the flat; the floodlight poles and the pillboxes trailed long, mournful shadows. There was a jeep waiting, and Ritchy-loo took the wheel himself.

We made a right turn around the corner of the building and then headed down one of the diagonal avenues between the poles. I glanced into the firing slit of one of the pillboxes as we passed it, and saw the gleam of somebody's spectacles.

"That was B building that we just came out of," said the captain. "Most of the interesting stuff is there, but you want to see everything, naturally, so we'll go over to C first and then back to A."

The huge barracks, far off to the right, looked deserted; I saw a few men in fatigues here and there, spearing stray bits of paper. Beyond the building we were heading for, almost against the wall, tiny figures were leaping rhythmically, opening and closing like so many animated scissors.

It was a well-policed area, at any rate; I watched for awhile, out of curiosity, and didn't see a single cigarette paper or gum wrapper.

To the left of the barracks and behind it was a miniature town—neat one-story cottages, all alike, all the same distance apart. The thing that struck me about it was that there were none of the signs of a permanent camp—no borders of whitewashed stones, no trees, no shrubs, no flowers. No *wives*, I thought.

"How's morale here, Captain?" I asked.

"Now, it's funny you should ask me that. That happens to be my job, I'm the Company B morale officer. Well, I should say that all things considered, we aren't doing too badly. Of course, we have a few difficulties. These men are here on eighteen-month assignments, and that's a kind of a long time without passes or furloughs. We'd like to make the hitches shorter, naturally, but of course you understand that there aren't too many fresh but seasoned troops available just now."

"No."

"But, we do our best. Now here's C building."

Most of C building turned out to be occupied by chemical laboratories long rows of benches covered by rank growths of glassware, only about a fifth of it working, and nobody watching more than a quarter of that.

"What are they doing here?"

"Over my head," said Ritchy-loo cheerfully. "Here's Dr. Vitale, let's ask him."

Vitale was a little sharp-featured man with a nervous blink. "This is the atmosphere section," he said. "We're trying to analyze the atmosphere which the alien breathes. Eventually we hope to manufacture it."

That was a point that hadn't occurred to me. "He can't breathe our air?"

"No, no. Altogether different."

"Well, where does he get the stuff he does breathe, then?"

The little man's lips worked. "From that cone-shaped mechanism on the top of his head. An atmosphere plant that you could put in your pocket. Completely incredible. We can't get an adequate sample without taking it off him, and we can't take it off him without killing him. We have to deduce what he breathes *in* from what he breathes *out. Very* difficult." He went away.

All the same, I couldn't see much point in it. Presumably if Aza-Kra couldn't breathe our air, we couldn't breathe his— so anybody who wanted to examine him would have to wear an oxygen tank and a breathing mask.

But it was obvious enough, and I got it in another minute. If the prisoner didn't have his own air-supply, it would be that much harder for him to break out past the gun-rooms and the guards in the corridors and the pillboxes and the floodlights and the wall...

We went on, stopping at every door. There were storerooms, sleeping quarters, a few offices. The rest of the rooms were empty.

Ritchy-loo wanted to go on to A building, but I was being perversely thorough, and I said we would go through the barracks and the company towns first. We did; it took us three hours, and thinned down Ritchy-loo's stream of cheerful conversation to a trickle. We looked everywhere and of course we did not find anything that shouldn't have been there.

A building was the recreation hall. Canteen, library, gymnasium, movie theater, PX, swimming pool. It was also the project hospital and dispensary. Both sections were well filled.

So we went back to B. And it was almost noon, so we had lunch in the big air-conditioned cafeteria. I didn't look forward to it; I expected that rest and food would turn on Ritchy-loo's conversational spigot again, and if he didn't get any response to the first three or four general topics he tried, I was perfectly sure he would begin telling me jokes.

Nothing of the kind happened. After a few minutes I saw why, or thought I did. Looking around the room, I saw face after face with the same blank look on it; there wasn't a smile or an animated expression in the place. And now that I was paying attention I noticed that the sounds were odd, too. There were more than a hundred people in the room, enough to set up a beehive roar; but there was so little talking going on that you could pick out individual sentences with ease, and they were all trochaic—*Want* some *su*gar? *No,* thanks. Like that.

It was infectious; I was beginning to feel it now myself, an execution-chamber kind of mood, a feeling that we were all shut up in a place that we couldn't get out of, find where something horrible was going to happen. Unless you've ever

131

been in a group made up of people who had that feeling and were reinforcing it in each other, it's indescribable; but it was very real and very hard to take.

Ritchy-loo left half a chop on his plate; I finished mine, but it choked me.

In the corridor outside I asked him, "Is it always as bad as that?"

"You noticed it too? That place gives me the creeps. I don't know why. It's the same way in the movies, too, lately—wherever you get a lot of these people together. I just don't understand it." For a second longer he looked worried and thoughtful, and then he grinned suddenly, "I don't want to say anything against civilians, Mr. Dahl, but I think that bunch is pretty far gone."

I could have hugged him.

Civilians! If Ritchy-loo was more than six months away from a summer-camp counselor's job, I was a five-star general.

We started at that end of the corridor and worked our way down. We looked into a room with an X-ray machine and a fluoroscope in it, and a darkroom, and a room full of racks and filing cabinets, and a long row of offices.

Then Ritchy-loo opened a door that revealed two men standing on opposite sides of a desk, spouting angry German at each other. The tall one noticed us after a second, said, "'St, 'st," to the other, and then to us, coldly. "You might, at least, knock."

"Sorry, gentlemen," said Ritchy-loo brightly. He closed the door and went on to the next on the same side. This opened onto a small, bare room with nobody in it but a stocky man with corporal's stripes on his sleeve. He was sitting hunched over; elbows on knees, hands over his face. He didn't move or look up.

I have a good ear, and I had managed to catch one sentence of what the fat man next door had been saying to the tall one. It went like this: "Nein, nein, das ist bestimmt nicht die Klaustrophobie; Ich sage dir, es ist das dreifüssige Tier, das sie stört."

My college German came back to me when I prodded it, but it creaked a little. While I was still working at it, I asked Ritchy-loo, "What was that?"

"Psychiatric section," he said.

"You get many psycho cases here?"

"Oh, no," he said. "Just the normal percentage, Mr. Dahl. Less, in fact."

The captain was a poor liar.

"Klaustrophobie" was easy, of course. "Dreifussige Tier" stopped me until I remembered that the German for "zoo" is "Tiergarten." Dreifüssige Tier: the three-footed beast. The tri-ped.

The fat one had been saying to the tall one, "No, no, it is absolutely not claustrophobia; I tell you, it's the tri-ped that's disturbing them."

Three-quarters of an hour later we had peered into the last room in B building: a long office full of IBM machines. We had now been over every square yard of Chillicothe, and I had seen for myself that no skullduggery was going forward anywhere in it. That was the idea behind the guided tour, as Ritchy-loo was evidently aware.

He said, "Well, that just about wraps it up, Mr. Dahl. By the way, the General's office asked me to tell you that if it's all right with you, they'll set up that phone call for you for four o'clock this afternoon."

I looked down at the rough map of the building I'd been drawing as we went along. "There's one place we haven't been, Captain," I said. "Section One."

"Oh, well that's right, that's right. You saw that yesterday, though, didn't you, Mr. Dahl?"

"For about two minutes. I wasn't able to take much of it in. I'd like to see it again, if it isn't too much trouble. Or—even if it is."

Ritchy-loo laughed heartily. "Good enough. Just wait a second. I'll see if I can get you a clearance on it." He walked down the corridor to the nearest wall phone.

After a few moments he beckoned me over, palming the receiver. "The General says there are two research groups in there now and it would be a little crowded. He says he'd like you to postpone it if you think you can."

"Tell him that's perfectly all right, but in that case I think we'd better put off the phone call, too."

He repeated the message, and waited. Finally, "Yes. Yes, uh-huh. Yes, I've got that. All right."

He turned to me. "The General says it's all right for you to go in for half an hour and watch, but he'd appreciate it if you'll be careful not to distract the people who're working in there."

I had been hoping the General would say no, I wanted to see the alien again, all right, but what I wanted the most was time.

This was the second day I had been at Chillicothe. By tomorrow at the latest I would have to talk to Eli Freeman; and I still hadn't figured out any sure, safe way to tell him that Chillicothe was a legitimate research project, not to be sniped at by the *Herald-Star*—and make him understand that I didn't mean a word of it.

I could simply refuse to make the call, or I could tell him as much of the truth as I could before I was cut off—two words, probably—but it was a cinch that call would be monitored at the other end, too; that was part of what Ritchy-loo meant by "setting up the call." Somebody from the FBI would be sitting at Freeman's elbow, and I wasn't telling myself fairy tales about Peter Zenger any more.

They would shut the paper down, which was not only the thing I wanted least in the world but a thing that would do nobody any good.

I wanted Eli to spread the story by underground channels—spread it so far, and time the release so well, that no amount of censorship could kill it.

Treason is a word every man has to define for himself.

Ritchy-loo did the honors for me at the gun-room door, and then left me, looking a little envious. I don't think he had ever been inside Section One.

There was somebody ahead of me in the tiny antechamber, I found: a short, wide-shouldered man with a sheep-dog tangle of black hair.

He turned as the door closed behind me. "Hi. Oh—you're Dahl, aren't you?" He had a young, pleasant, meaningless face behind dark-rimmed glasses. I said yes.

He put a half-inch of cigarette between his lips and shook hands with me. "Somebody pointed you out. Glad to know you; my name's Donnelly. Physical psych section—very junior." He pointed through the spy-window. "What do you think of him?"

Aza-Kra was sitting directly in front of the window; his lunch-counter stool had been moved into the center of the room. Around him were four men: two on the left, sitting on folding chairs, talking to him and occasionally making notes; two on the right, standing beside a waist-high enclosed mechanism from which wires led to the upper lobe of the alien's body. The ends of the wires were taped against his skin.

"That isn't an easy question," I said.

Donnelly nodded without interest. "That's my boss there," he said, "the skinny, gray-haired guy on the right. We get on each other's nerves. If he gets that setup operating this session, I'm supposed to go in and take notes. He won't, though."

"What is it?"

"Electroencephalograph. See, his brain isn't in his head, it's in his upper thorax there. Too much insulation in the way. We can't get close enough for a good reading without surgery. I say we ought to drop it till we get permission, but Hendricks thinks he can lick it. Those two on the other side are interviewers. Like to hear what they're saying?"

He punched one of two buttons set into the door beside the speaker grill, under the spy window. "If you're ever in here alone, remember you can't get out while this is on. You turn on the speaker here, it turns off the one in the gun-room. They wouldn't be able to hear you ask to get out."

Inside, a monotonous voice was saying, "...have that here, but what exactly do you mean by..."

"I ought to be in physiology," Donnelly said, lowering his voice. "They have all the fun. You see his eyes?"

I looked. The center one was staring directly toward us; the other two were tilted, almost out of sight around the curve of that bulb of blue-gray flesh.

"...in other words, just what is the nature of this energy, is it—uh—transmitted by waves, or..."

"He can look three ways at once," I said.

"Three, with binocular," Donnelly agreed. "Each eye can function independently or couple with the one on either side. So he can have a series of overlapping monocular images, all the way around, or he can have up to three binocular images. They focus independently, too. He could read a newspaper and watch for his wife to come out of the movie across the street."

"Wait a minute," I said. "He has *six* eyes, not three?"

"Sure. Has to, to keep the symmetry and still get binocular vision."

"Then he hasn't got any front or back," I said slowly.

"No, that's right. He's trilaterally symmetrical. Drive you crazy to watch him walk. His legs work the same way as his eyes—anyone can pair up with either of the others. He wants to change direction, he doesn't have to turn around. I'd hate to try to catch him in an open field."

"How did they catch him?" I asked.

"Luckiest thing in the world. Found him in the woods with two broken ankles. Now look at his hands. What do you see?"

The voice inside was still droning; evidently it was a long question. "Five fingers," I said.

"Nope." Donnelly grinned. "One finger, four thumbs. See how they oppose, those two on either side of the middle finger? He's got a better hand than ours. One *hell* of an efficient design. Brain in his thorax where it's safe, six eyes on a stalk—trachea up there too, no connection with the esophagus, so he doesn't need an epiglottis. Three of everything else. He can lose a leg and still walk, lose an arm and still type, lose two eyes and still see better than we do. He can lose—"

I didn't hear him. The interviewer's voice had stopped, and Aza-Kra's had begun. It was frightening, because it was a buzzing and it was voice.

I couldn't take in a word of it; I had enough to do absorbing the fact that there were words.

Then it stopped, and the interviewer's ordinary, flat Middle Western voice began again. "—And just try to sneak up behind him," said Donnelly. "I dare you."

Again Aza-Kra spoke briefly, and this time I saw the flesh at the side of his body, where the two lobes flowed together, bulge slightly and then relax.

"He's talking with one of his mouths," I said. "I mean, one of those—" I took a deep breath. "If he breathes through the top of his head, and there's no connection between his lungs and his vocal organs, then where the hell does he get the air?"

"He belches. Not as inconvenient as it sounds. You could learn to do it if you had to." Donnelly laughed. "Not very fragrant, though. Watch their faces when he talks."

I watched Aza-Kra's instead—what there was of it: one round, expressionless, oyster-colored eye staring back at me. With a human opponent, I was thinking, there were a thousand little things that you relied on to help you: facial expressions, mannerisms, signs of emotion. But Parst had been right when he said, *There isn't a single possibility we can rule out. Not one.* And so had the fat man: *It's the tri-ped that's disturbing them.* And Ritchy-loo: *It's the same way...wherever you get a lot of these people together.*

And I still hadn't figured out any way to tell Freeman what he had to know.

I thought I could arouse Eli's suspicion easily enough; we knew each other well enough for a word or a gesture to mean a good deal. I could make him look for hidden meanings. But how could I hide a message so that Eli would be more likely to dig it out than a trained FBI cryptologist?

I stared at Aza-Kra's glassy eye as if the answer were there. It was going to be a video circuit, I told myself. Donnelly was still yattering in my ear, and now the alien was buzzing again, but I ignored them both. Suppose I broke the message up into one-word units, scattered them through my conversation with Eli, and marked them off somehow—by twitching a finger, or blinking my eyelids?

A dark membrane flicked across the alien's oyster-colored eye.

A moment later, it happened again.

Donnelly was saying, "...intercoastal membranes, apparently. But there's no trace of..."

"Shut up a minute, will you?" I said. "I want to hear this."

The inhuman voice, the voice that sounded like the articulate buzzing of a giant insect, was saying, "Comparison not possible, excuse me. If *(blink)* you try to understand in words you know, you *(blink)* tell yourself you wish *(blink)* to understand, but knowledge escape *(blink)* you. Can only show *(blink)* you from beginning, one *(blink)* little, another little. Not possible to carry all knowledge in one hand *(blink)*."

If you wish escape, show one hand.

I looked at Donnelly. He had moved back from the spy-window; he was lighting a cigarette, frowning at the match-flame. His mouth was sullen.

I put my left hand flat against the window. I thought, *I'm dreaming.*

The interviewer said querulously, "—getting us nowhere. Can't you—"

"Wait," said the buzzing voice. "Let me say, please. Ignorant man hold *(blink)* burning stick, say, this is breath *(blink)* of the wood. Then you show him flashlight—"

I took a deep breath, and held it.

Around the alien, four men went down together, folding over quietly at waist and knee, sprawling on the floor. I heard a thump behind me.

Donnelly was lying stretched out along the wall, his head tilted against the corner. The cigarette had fallen from his hand.

I looked back at Aza-Kra. His head turned slightly, the dark flesh crinkling. Two eyes stared back at me through the window.

"Now you can breathe," said the monster.

CHAPTER THREE

I let out the breath that was choking me and took another. My knees were shaking.

"What did you do to them?"

"Put them to sleep only. In a few minutes I will put the others to sleep. After you are outside the doors. First we will talk."

I glanced at Donnelly again. His mouth was ajar; I could see his lips fluttering as he breathed.

"All right," I said, "talk."

"When you leave," buzzed the voice, "you must take me with you."

Now it was clear. He could put people to sleep, but he couldn't open locked doors. He had to have help.

"No deal," I said. "You might as well knock me out, too."

"Yes," he answered, "you will do it. When you understand."

"I'm listening."

"You do not have to agree now. I ask only this much. When we are finished talking, you leave. When you are past the second door, hold your breath again. Then go to the office of General Parst. You will find their papers about me. Read them. You will find also keys to open gun-room. Also, handcuffs. Special handcuffs, made to fit me. Then you will think, if Aza-Kra is not what he says, would he agree to this? Then you will come back to gun-room, use controls there to open middle door. You will lay handcuffs down, where you stand now, then go back to gun-room, open inside door. I will put on the handcuffs you will see that I do it. And then you will take me with you."

I said, "Let me think."

The obvious thing to do was to push the little button that turned on the audio circuit to the gun-room, and yell for help; the alien could then put everybody to sleep from here to the wall, maybe, but it wouldn't do any good. Sooner or later he would have to let up, or starve to death along with the rest of us. On the other hand if I did what he asked—*anything* he asked—and it turned out to be the wrong thing, I would be guilty of the worst crime since Pilate's.

But I thought about it, I went over it again and again, and I couldn't see any loophole in it for Aza-Kra. He was leaving it up to me—if I felt like letting him out after I'd seen the papers in Parst's office, I could do so. If I didn't, I could still yell for help. In fact, I could get on the phone and yell to Washington, which would be a hell of a lot more to the point.

So where was the payoff for Aza-Kra? What was in those papers?

I pushed the button, I said, "This is Dahl. Let me out, will you please?"

The outer door began to slide back. Just in time, I saw Donnelly's head bobbing against it; I grabbed him by the shirtfront and hoisted his limp body out of the way.

I walked across the echoing outer chamber; the outermost door opened for me. I stepped through it and held my breath.

Down the corridor, three guards leaned over their rifles and toppled all in a row, like precision divers. Beyond them a hurrying civilian in the cross-corridor fell heavily and skidded out of sight.

The clacking of typewriters from a nearby office had stopped abruptly. I let out my breath when I couldn't hold it any longer, and listened to the silence.

The General was slumped over his desk, head on his crossed forearms, looking pretty old and tired with his polished bald skull shining under the light. There was a faint silvery scar running across the top of his head, and I wondered whether he had got it in combat as a young man, or whether he had tripped over a rug at an embassy reception.

Across the desk from him a thin man in a gray pin-check suit was jackknifed on the carpet, half-supported by a chair-leg, rump higher than his head.

There were two six-foot filing cabinets in the right-hand corner behind the desk. Both were locked; the drawers of the first one were labeled alphabetically, the other was unmarked.

I unhooked Parst's key-chain from his belt. He had as many keys as a janitor or a high school principal, but not many of them were small enough to fit the filing cabinets. I got the second one unlocked and began going through the drawers. I found what I wanted in the top one—seven fat manila folders labeled "Aza-Kra—Armor," "Aza-Kra—General information," "Aza-Kra—Power sources," "Aza-Kra—Space-flight" and so on; and one more labeled "Directives and related correspondence."

I hauled them all out, piled them on Parst's desk and pulled up a chair.

I took "Armor" first because it was on top and because the title puzzled me. The folder was full of transcripts of interview whose subject I had to work out as I went along. It appeared that when captured, Aza-Kra had been wearing a light-weight bullet-proof body armor, made of something that was longitudinally flexible and perpendicularly rigid—in other words, you could pull it on like a suit of winter underwear, but you couldn't dent it with a sledge hammer.

They had been trying to find out what the stuff was and how it was made for almost two months and as far as I could see they had not made a nickel's worth of progress.

I looked through "Power sources" and "Spaceflight" to see if they were the same, and they were. The odd part was that Aza-Kra's answers didn't sound reluctant or evasive; but he kept running into ideas for which there weren't any words in English and then they would have to start all over again, like Twenty Questions. Is it animal? vegetable? mineral? It was a mess.

I put them all aside except "General information" and Directives." The first, as I had guessed, was a catch-all for non-technical subjects—where Aza-Kra had come from, what his people were like, his reasons for coming to this planet: all the unimportant questions; or the only questions that had any importance, depending on how you looked at it.

Parst had already given me an accurate summary of it, but it was surprisingly effective in Aza-Kra's words. *You say we want your planet. There are many planets, so many you would not believe. But if we wanted your planet, and if we could kill as you do, please understand, we are very many. We would fall on your planet like snowflakes. We would not send one man alone.*

And later : *Most young peoples kill. It is a law of nature, yes, but try to understand, it is not the only law. You have been a young people, but now you are growing older. Now you must learn the other law, not to kill. That is what I have come to teach. Until you learn this, we cannot have you among us.*

There was nothing in the folder dated later than a month and a half ago. They had dropped that line of questioning early.

The first thing I saw in the other folder began like this:
You are hereby directed to hold yourself in readiness to destroy the subject under any of the following circumstances, without further specific notification:

1. a: If the subject attempts to escape.

1. b: If the subject kills or injures a human being.

1. c: If the landing, anywhere in the world, of other members of the subject's race is reported and their similarity to the subject established beyond a reasonable doubt...

Seeing it written down like that, in the cold dead-aliveness of black words on white paper, it was easy to forget that the alien was a stomach-turning monstrosity, and to see only that what he had to say was lucid and noble.

But I still hadn't found anything that would persuade me to help him escape. The problem was still there, as insoluble as ever. There was no way of evaluating a word the alien said about himself. He had come alone—perhaps—instead of bringing an invading army with him; but how did we know that one member of his race wasn't as dangerous to us as Perry's battleship to the Japanese? He might be; there was some evidence that he was.

My quarrel with the Defense Department was not that they were mistreating an innocent three-legged missionary, but simply that the problem of Aza-Kra belonged to the world, not to a fragment of the executive branch of the Government of the United States—and certainly not to me.

...There was one other way out, I realized. Instead of calling Frisbee in Washington, I could call an arm-long list of senators and representatives. I could call the UN secretariat in New York; I could call the editor of every major newspaper in this hemisphere and the head of every wire service and broadcasting chain. I could stir up a hornet's nest, even, as the saying goes, if I swung for it.

Wrong again: I couldn't. I opened the "Directives" folder again, looking for what I thought I had seen there in the list of hypothetical circumstances. There it was:

1. f: If any concerted attempt on the part of any person or group to remove the subject from Defense Department custody, or to aid him in any way, is made; or if the subject's existence and presence in Defense Department custody becomes public knowledge.

That sewed it up tight, and it also answered my question about Aza-Kra. Knocking out the personnel of B building would be construed as an attempt to escape or as a concerted attempt by a person or group to remove the subject from Defense Department custody, it didn't matter which. If I broke the story, it would have the same result. They would kill him.

In effect, he had put his life in my hands: and that was why he was so sure that I'd help him.

It might have been that, or what I found just before I left the office, that decided me. I don't know; I wish I did.

Coming around the desk the other way, I glanced at the thin man on the floor and noticed that there was something under him, half-hidden by his body. It turned out to be two things: a gray fedora and a pint-sized gray-leather briefcase, chained to his wrist.

So I looked under Parst's folded arms, saw the edge of a thick white sheet of paper, and pulled it out.

Under Frisbee's letterhead, it said:

> *By courier.*
> *Dear General Parst:*
> *Some possibility appears to exist that A.K. is responsible for recent disturbances in your area; please give me your thought on this as soon as possible—the decision can't be long postponed.*
>
> *In the meantime you will of course consider your command under emergency status, and we count on you to use your initiative to safeguard security at all costs. In a crisis, you will consider Lieut. D. as expendable.*
>
> *Sincerely yours,*
> *Carlton Frisbee*
> *cf/ cf/ enc.*

"Enc." meant "enclosure." I pried up Parst's arms again and found another sheet of stiff paper, folded three times, with a paperclip on it.

It was a First Lieutenant's commission, made out to Robert James Dahl, dated three days before, with a perfect forgery of my signature at the bottom of it.

If commissions can be forged, so can court-martial records.

I put the commission and the letter in my pocket, I didn't seem to feel any particular emotion, but I noticed that my hands were shaking as I sorted through the "General information" file, picked out a few sheets and stuffed them into my pocket with the other papers. I wasn't confused or in doubt about what to do next. I looked around the room, spotted a metal locker diagonally across from the filing cabinets, and opened it with one of the General's keys.

Inside were two .45 automatics, boxes of ammunition, several loaded clips, and three odd-looking sets of handcuffs, very wide and heavy, each with its key.

I took the handcuffs, the keys, both automatics and all the clips.

In a storeroom at the end of the corridor I found a two-wheeled dolly, I wheeled it all the way around to Section One and left it outside the center door. Then it struck me that I was still wearing the pinks they had given me when I arrived, and where the hell were my own clothes? I took a chance and went up to my room on the second floor, remembering that I hadn't been back there since morning.

There they were, neatly laid out on the bed. My keys, lighter, change, wallet and, so on were on the bedside table. I changed and went back down to Section One.

In the gun-room were two sprawled shapes, one beside the machine-gun that poked its snout through the hemispherical blister, the other under a panel set with three switches and, a microphone.

The switches were clearly marked. I opened, the first two, walked out and around and laid the three sets of handcuffs on the floor in the middle room. Then I went back to the gunroom, closed the first two doors and opened the third.

Soft thumping sounds came from the loudspeaker over the switch panel; then the rattling of metal, more thumps, and finally a series of rattling clicks.

I opened the first door and went back inside. Through the panel in the middle door I could see Aza-Kra; he had retreated into the inner room so that all of him was plainly visible. He was squatting on the floor, his legs drawn up. His arms were at full stretch, each wrist manacled to an ankle. He strained his arms outward to show me that the cuffs were tight.

I made one more trip to open the middle door. Then I got the dolly and wheeled it in.

"Thank you," said Aza-Kra. I got a whiff of his "breath" as Donnelly had intimated, it wasn't pleasant.

Halfway to the airport, at Aza-Kra's request, I held my breath again. Aside from that we didn't speak except when I asked him, as I was loading him from the jeep into a limousine, "How long will they stay unconscious?"

"Not more than twenty hours, I think. I could have given them more, but I did not dare, I do not know your chemistry well enough."

We could go a long way in twenty hours. We would certainly have to.

I hated to go home, it was too obvious and there was a good chance that the hunt would start before any twenty hours were up, but there wasn't any help for it. I had a passport and a visa for England, where I had been planning to go for a publishers' conference in January, but it hadn't occurred to me to take it along on a quick trip to Washington. And now I had to have the passport.

My first idea had been to head for New York and hand Aza-Kra over to the UN there, but I saw it was no good. Extraterritoriality was just a word, like a lot of other words; we wouldn't be safe until we were out of the country, and on second thought, maybe not then.

It was a little after eight-thirty when I pulled in to the curb down the street from my house. I hadn't eaten since noon, but I wasn't hungry; and it didn't occur to me until later to think about Aza-Kra.

I got the passport and some money without waking my housekeeper. A few blocks away I parked again on a side street, I called the airport, got a reservation on the next eastbound flight, and spent half an hour buying a trunk big enough for Aza-Kra and wrestling him into it.

It struck me at the last minute that perhaps I had been counting too much on that atmosphere-plant of his. His air supply was taken care of, but what about his respiratory waste produced—would he poison himself in that tiny closed space? I asked him, and he said, "No, it is all right. I will be warm, but I can bear it."

I put the lid down, then opened it again. "I forgot about food," I said. "What do you eat, anyway?"

"At Chillicothe I ate soya bean extract. With added minerals. But I am able to go without food for long periods. Please, do not worry."

All right. I put the lid down again and locked the trunk, but I didn't stop worrying.

He was being too accommodating.

I had expected him to ask me to turn him loose, or take him to wherever his spaceship was. He hadn't brought the subject up; he hadn't even asked me where we were going, or what my plans were.

I thought I knew the answer to that, but it didn't make me any happier. He didn't ask, because he already knew—just as he'd known the contents of Parst's office, down to the last document; just as he'd known what I was thinking when I was in the anteroom with Donnelly.

He read minds. And he gassed people through solid metal walls.

What else did he do?

There wasn't time to dispose of the limousine; I simply left it at the airport. If the alarm went out before we got to the coast, we were sunk anyhow; if not, it wouldn't matter.

Nobody stopped us. I caught the stratojet in New York at 12:20, and five hours later we were in London.

Customs was messy, but there wasn't any other way to handle it. When we were fifth in line, I thought: *Knock them out for about an hour*—and held my breath. Nothing happened. I rapped on the side of the trunk to attract his attention, and did it again. This time it worked: everybody in sight went down like a rag doll.

I stamped my own passport, filled out a declaration form and buried it in a stack of others, put a tag on the trunk, loaded it aboard a hand truck, wheeled it outside and took a cab.

I had learned something in the process, although it certainly wasn't much: either Aza-Kra couldn't, or didn't, eavesdrop on my mind all the time—or else he was simply one step ahead of me.

Later, on the way to the harbor, I saw a newsstand and realized that it was going on three days since I had seen a paper. I had tried to get the New York dailies at the airport, but they'd been sold out—nothing on the stands but a lone copy of the Staten Island *Advance*. That hadn't struck me as odd at the time—an index of my state of mind—but it did now.

I got out and bought a copy of everything on the stand except the tipsheets—four newspapers, all of them together about equaling the bulk of one *Herald-Star*. I felt frustrated enough to ask the newsvendor if he had any papers left over from yesterday or the day before. He gave me a glassy look, made me repeat it, then pulled his face into an indescribable expression, laid a finger beside his nose, and said, "'Arf a mo.'" He scuttled into a bar a few yards down the street, was gone five minutes, and came back clutching a mare's-nest of soiled and bedraggled papers.

"'Ere you are, guvner. Three bob for the lot."

I paid him. "Thanks," I said, "very much."

He waved his hand expansively. "Okay, bud," he said. "T'ink nuttin' of it!"

A comedian.

The only Channel boat leaving before late afternoon turned out to be an excursion steamer-round trip, two guineas. The boat wasn't crowded; it was the tag end of the season, and a rough, windy day. I found a seat without any trouble and finished sorting out my stack of papers by date and folio.

British newspapers don't customarily report any more of our news than we do of theirs, but this week our supply of catastrophes had been ample enough to make good reading across the Atlantic. I found all three of the Chicago stories— trimmed to less than two inches apiece, but there. I read the first with professional interest, the second skeptically, and the third with alarm.

I remembered the run of odd items I'd read in that Washington hotel room, a long time ago. I remembered

Frisbee's letter to Parst : *"Some possibility appears to exist that A. K. is responsible for recent disturbances in your area..."*

I found two of the penitentiary stories, half smothered by stop press, and I added them to the total. I drew an imaginary map of the United States in my head and stuck imaginary pins in it. Red ones, a little cluster: Des Moines, Kansas City, Decatur, St. Louis. Blue ones, a scattering around them: Chicago, Leavenworth, Terre Haute.

Down toward the end of the cabin someone's portable radio was muttering.

A fat youth in a checkered jacket had it. He moved over reluctantly and made room for me to sit down. The crisp, controlled BBC voice was saying, "...in Commons today, declared that Britain's trade balance is more favorable than at any time during the past fifteen years. In London, ceremonies marking the sixth anniversary of the death..." I let the words slide past me until I heard:

"In the United States, the mysterious epidemic affecting stockyard workers in the central states has spread to New York and New Jersey on the eastern seaboard. The President has requested Congress to provide immediate emergency meat-rationing legislation."

A blurred little woman on the bench opposite leaned forward and said, "Serve 'em right, too! Them with their beefsteak a day."

There were murmurs of approval.

I got up and went back to my own seat. It all fell into one pattern, everything: the man who kicked his wife, the prize-fighters, the policeman, the wardens, the slaughterhouse "epidemic."

It was the lex talionis—or the Golden Rule in reverse: Be done by as you do to others.

When you injured another living thing, both of you felt the same pain. When you killed, you felt the shock of your victim's death. You might be only stunned by it, like the slaughterhouse workers, or you might die, like the policeman and the schoolboy murderer.

So-called mental anguish counted too, apparently. That explained the wave of humanitarianism in prisons, at least partially; the rest was religious hysteria and the kind of herd-instinct that makes any startling new movement mushroom.

And, of course, it also explained Chillicothe: the horrible blanketing depression that settled anywhere the civilian staff congregated—the feeling of being penned up in a place where something frightful was going to happen—and the thing the two psychiatrists had been arguing about, the pseudo-claustrophobia...all that was nothing but the reflection of Aza-Kra's feelings, locked in that cell on an alien planet.

Be done by as you do.

And I was carrying that with me. Des Moines, Kansas City, Decatur, St. Louis, Chicago, Leavenworth, Terre Haute—*New York.* After that, England. We'd been in London less than an hour—but England is only four hundred-odd miles long, from Spittal to Lands End.

I remembered what Aza-Kra had said: *Now you must learn the other law, not to kill.*

Not to kill tri-peds.

My body was shaking uncontrollably; my head felt like a balloon stuffed with cotton. I stood up and looked around at the blank faces, the inward-looking eyes, every man, woman and child living in a little world of his own. I had an hysterical impulse to shout at them, *Look at you, you idiots! You've been invaded and half conquered without a shot fired, and you don't know it!*

In the next instant I realized that I was about to burst into laughter. I put my hand over my mouth and half-ran out on deck, giggles leaking through my fingers; I got to the rail and bent myself over it, roaring apoplectic. I was utterly ashamed of myself, but I couldn't stop it; it was like a fit of vomiting.

The cold spray on my face sobered me. I leaned over the rail, looking down at the white water boiling along the hull. It occurred to me that there was one practical test still to be made: a matter of confirmation.

A middle-aged man with rheumy eyes was standing in the cabin doorway, partly blocking it. As I shouldered past him, I deliberately put my foot down on his.

An absolutely blinding pain shot through the toes of my right foot. When my eyes cleared I saw that the two of us were standing in identical attitudes—weight on one foot, the other knee bent, hand reaching instinctively for the injury. I had taken him for a "typical Englishman," but he cursed me in a rattling stream of gutter French. I apologized: awkwardly but sincerely—very sincerely.

When we docked at Dunkirk I still hadn't decided what to do. What I had had in mind up till now was simply to get across France into Switzerland and hold a press conference there, inviting everybody from Tass to the UP. It had to be Switzerland for fairly obvious reasons; the English or the French would clamp a security lid on me before you could say NATO, but the Swiss wouldn't dare—they paid for their neutrality by having to look *both* ways before they cleared their throats.

I could still do that, and let the UN set up a committee to worry about Aza-Kra—but at a conservative estimate it would be ten months before the committee got its foot out of its mouth, and that would be pretty nearly ten months too late.

Or I could simply go to the American consulate in Dunkirk and turn myself in. Within ten hours we would be back in Chillicothe, probably, and I'd be free of the responsibility. I would also be dead.

We got through customs the same way we'd done in London.

And then I had to decide.

The cab driver put his engine in gear and looked at me over his shoulder. "Un hôtel?"

"...Yes," I said. "A cheap hotel. Un hôtel à bon marchè."

"Entendu." He jammed down the accelerator an instant before he let out the clutch; we were doing thirty before he shifted into second.

The place he took me to was a villainous third-rate commercial travelers' hotel, smelling of urine and dirty linen. When the porters were gone I unlocked the trunk and opened it.

We stared at each other.

Moisture was beaded on his blue-gray skin, and there was a smell in the room stronger and ranker than anything that belonged there. His eyes looked duller than they had before; I could barely see the pupils.

"Well?" I said.

"You are half right," he buzzed. "I am doing it, but not for the reason you think."

"All right; you're doing it. *Stop it.* That comes first. We'll stay here, and I'll watch the papers to make sure you do."

"At the customs, those people will sleep only an hour."

"I don't give a damn. If the gendarmes come up here, you can put them to sleep. If I have to I'll move you out to the country and we'll live under a haystack. But no matter what happens we're not going a mile farther into Europe until I know you've quit. If you don't like that, you've got two choices. Either you knock me out, and see how much good it does you, or I'll take that air-machine off your head."

He buzzed inarticulately for a moment. Then, "I have to say no. It is impossible, I could stop for a time, or pretend to you that I stop, but that would solve nothing. It will be—it will do the greatest harm if I stop; you don't understand. It is necessary to continue."

I said, "That's your answer?"

"Yes. If you will let me explain—"

I stepped toward him. I didn't hold my breath, but I think half-consciously I expected him to gas me. He didn't. He didn't move; he just waited.

Seen at close range, the flesh of his head seemed to be continuous with the black substance of the cone; instead of any sharp dividing line, there was a thin area that was neither one nor the other.

I put one hand over the fleshy bulb, and felt his eyes retract and close against my palm. The sensation was indescribably unpleasant, but I kept my hand there, put the other one against the far side of the cone—pulled and pushed simultaneously, as hard as I could.

The top of my head came off.

I was leaning against the top of the open trunk, dizzy and nauseated. The pain was like a white-hot wire drawn tight around my skull just above the eyes. I couldn't see; I couldn't think.

And it didn't stop; it went on and on... I pushed myself away from the trunk and let my legs fold under me. I sat on the floor with my head in my hands, pushing my fingers against the pain.

Gradually it ebbed. I heard Aza-Kra's voice buzzing very quietly, not in English but in a rhythm of tone and phrasing that seemed almost directly comprehensible; if there were a language designed to be spoken by bass viols, it might sound like that.

I got up and looked at him. Shining beads of blue liquid stood out all along the base of the cone, but the seam had not broken.

I hadn't realized that it would be so difficult, that it would be so painful. I felt the weight of the two automatics in my pockets, and I pulled one out, the metal cold and heavy in my palm, but I knew suddenly that I couldn't do that either.

I didn't know where his brain was, or his heart. I didn't know whether I could kill him with one shot.

I sat down on the bed, staring at him. "You knew that would happen, didn't you," I said. "You must think I'm a prize sucker."

He said nothing. His eyes were half-closed, and a thin whey-colored fluid was drooling out of the two mouths I could see. Aza-Kra was being sick.

I felt an answering surge of nausea. Then the flow stopped, and a second later the nausea stopped too. I felt angry, and frustrated, and frightened.

After a moment I got up off the bed and started for the door.

"Please," said Aza-Kra. "Will you be gone long?"

"I don't know," I said. "Does it matter?"

"If you will be gone long," he said, "I would ask that you loosen the handcuffs for a short period before you go."

I stared at him, suddenly hating him with a violence that shook me.

"No," I said, and reached for the door-handle.

My body knotted itself together like a fist. My legs gave way under me, and I missed the door-handle going down: I hit the floor hard.

There was no sensation in my hands or feet. The muscles of my shoulders, arms, thighs and calves were one huge, heavy pain. And I couldn't move.

I looked at Aza-Kra's wrists, shackled to his drawn-up ankles. He had been like that for something like fourteen hours. He had cramps.

"I am sorry," said Aza-Kra. "I did not want to do that to you, but there was no other way."

I thought dazedly, *No other way to do what?*

"To make you wait. To listen. To let me explain."

I said, "I don't get it." Anger flared again, then faded under something more intense and painful. The closest English word for it is "humility," some other language may come nearer, but I doubt it, it isn't an emotion that we like to talk about. I felt bewildered, and ashamed, and very small, all at once, and there was another component, harder to name. A...threshold feeling.

I tried again. "I felt the other pain, before, but not this. Is that because—"

"Yes. There must be the intention to injure, or cause pain. I will tell you why. I have to go back very far. When an animal becomes more developed—many cells, instead of one—always the same things happen. I am the first man of my kind who ever saw a man of your kind. But we both have eyes. We both have ears." The feathery spines on his neck stiffened and relaxed. "Also there is another sense that always comes. But always it goes only a little way and then stops.

"When you are a young animal, fighting with the others to live, it is useful to have a sense which feels the thoughts of the enemy. Just as it is useful to have a sense which sees the shape of his body. But this sense cannot come all at once, it must grow by a little and a little, as when a surface that can tell the light from the dark becomes a true eye.

"But the easiest thoughts to feel are the pain thoughts, they are much stronger than any others. And when the sense

157

is still weak—it is a part of the brain, not an organ by itself—when it is weak, only the strongest stimulus can make it work. This stimulus is hatred, or anger, or the wish to kill.

"So that just when the sense is enough developed that it could begin to be useful, it always disappears. It is not gone, it is pushed under. A very long time ago, one race discovered this sense and learned how it could be brought back. It is done by a class of organic chemicals. You have not the word. For each race a different member of the class, but always it can be done. The chemical is a catalyst, it is not used up. The change it makes is in the cells of all the body—it is permanent, it passes also to the children.

"You understand, when a race is older, to kill is not useful. With the change, true civilization begins. The first race to find this knowledge gave it to others, and those to others, and now all have it. All who are able to leave their planets. We give it to you, now, because you are ready. When you are older, there will be others who are ready. You will give it to them."

While I had been listening, the pain in my arms and legs had slowly been getting harder and harder to take. I reminded myself that Aza-Kra had borne it, probably, at least ten hours longer than I had; but that didn't make it much easier. I tried to keep my mind off it but that wasn't possible; the band of pain around my head was still there, too, a faint throbbing. And both were consequences of things I had done to Aza-Kra. I was suffering with him, measure for measure.

Justice. Surely that was a good thing? Automatic instant retribution, mathematically accurate: an eye for an eye.

I said, "That was what you were doing when they caught you, then—finding out which chemical we reacted to?"

"Yes. I did not finish until after they had brought me to Chillicothe. Then it was much more difficult. If not for my accident, all would have gone much more quickly."

"The walls?"

"Yes. As you have guessed, my air machine will also make other substances and expel them with great force. Also, when necessary, it will place these substances in a—state of matter, you have not the word—so that they pass through solid objects. But this takes much power. While in Chillicothe my range was very small. Later, when I can be in the open, it will be much greater."

He caught what I was thinking before I had time to speak. He said, "Yes. You will agree. When you understand."

It was the same thing he had told me at Chillicothe, almost to the word.

I said, "You keep talking about this thing as a gift but I notice you didn't ask us if we wanted it. What kind of a gift is that?"

"You are not serious. You know what happened when I was captured."

After a moment he added, "I think if it had been possible, if we could have asked each man and woman on the planet to say yes or no, explaining everything, showing that there was no trick, that most would have said yes. For people the change is good. But for governments it is not good."

I said, "I'd like to believe you. It would be very pleasant to believe you. But nothing you can say changes the fact that this thing, this gift of yours could be a weapon. To soften us up before you move in. If you were an advance agent for an invasion fleet, this is what you'd be doing."

"You are thinking with habits," he said. "Try to think with logic. Imagine that your race is very old, with much knowledge. You have ships that cross between the stars. Now you discover this young race, these Earthmen, who only begin to learn to leave their own planet. You decide to conquer them. Why? What is your reason?"

"How do I know? It could be anything. It might be something I couldn't even imagine. For all I know you want to eat us."

His throat-spines quivered. He said slowly, "You are partly serious. You really think... I am sorry that you did not read the studies of the physiologists. If you had, you would know. My digestion is only for vegetable food. You cannot understand, but with us, to eat meat is like with you, to eat excretions."

I said, "All right, maybe we have something else you want. Natural resources that you've used up. Some substance, maybe some rare element."

"This is still habit thinking. Have you forgotten my air machine?"

"—Or maybe you just want the planet itself. With us cleared off it, to make room for you."

"Have you never looked at the sky at night?"

I said, "All *right*. But this quiz was your idea, not mine. I *admit* that I don't know enough even to make a sensible guess at your motives. And that's the reason why I can't trust you."

He was silent a moment. Then: "Remember that the substance which makes the change is a catalyst. Also it is a very fine powder. The particles are of only a few molecules each. The winds carry it. It is swallowed and breathed in and absorbed by the skin. It is breathed out and excreted. The wind takes it again. Water carries it. It is carried by insects and by birds and animals, and by men, in their bodies and in their clothing.

"This you can understand and know that it is true. If I die another could come and finish what I have begun, but even this is not necessary. The amount of the catalyst I have already released is more than enough. It will travel slowly, but nothing can stop it. If I die now, this instant still in a year the catalyst will reach every part of the planet."

After a long time I said, "Then what did you mean by saying that a great harm would be done, if you stopped now?"

"I meant this. Until now, only your Western nations have the catalyst. In a few days their time of crisis will come, beginning with the United States. And the nations of the East will attack."

CHAPTER FOUR

I found that I could move, inchmeal, if I sweated hard enough at it. It took me what seemed like half an hour to get my hand into my pocket, paw all the stuff out onto the floor, and get the key ring hooked over one finger. Then I had to crawl about ten feet to Aza-Kra, and when I got there my fingers simply wouldn't hold the keys firmly enough.

I picked them up in my teeth and got two of the wristcuffs unlocked. That was the best I could do; the other one was behind him, inside the trunk, and neither of us had strength enough to pull him out where I could get at it.

It was comical. My muscles weren't cramped, but my nervous system was getting messages that said they were—so, to all intents and purposes, it was true. I had no control over it; the human body is about as skeptical as a God-smitten man at a revival meeting. If mine had thought it was burning, I would have developed simon-pure blisters.

Then the pins-and-needles started, as Aza-Kra began to flex his arms and legs to get the stiffness out of them. Between us, after awhile, we got him out of the trunk and unlocked the third cuff. In a few minutes I had enough freedom of movement to begin massaging his cramped muscles; but it was three-quarters of an hour before either of us could stand.

We caught the mid-afternoon plane to Paris, with Aza-Kra in the trunk again. I checked into a hotel, left him there, and went shopping: I bought a hideous black dress with imitation-onyx trimming, a black coat with a cape, a feather muff, a tall black hat and the heaviest mourning veil I could find. At a theatrical costumer's near the Place de l'Opera I got a reasonably lifelike old-woman mask and a heavy wig.

When he was dressed, up, the effect was startling. The tall hat covered the cone, the muff covered two of his hands. There was nothing to be done about the feet, but the skirt hung almost to the ground, and I thought he would pass, with luck.

We got a cab and headed for the American consulate, but halfway there I remembered about the photographs. We stopped off at an amusement arcade and I got my picture taken in a coin-operated machine. Aza-Kra was another problem—that mask wouldn't fool anybody without the veil—but I spotted a poorly dressed old woman and with some difficulty managed to make her understand that I was a crazy American who would pay her five hundred francs to pose for her picture. We struck a bargain at a thousand.

As soon as we got into the consulate waiting room, Aza-Kra gassed everybody in the building. I locked the street door and searched the offices until I found a man with a little pile of blank passport books on the desk in front of him. He had been filling one in on a machine like a typewriter except that it had a movable plane-surface platen instead of a cylinder.

I moved him out of the way and made out two passports: one for myself, as Arthur James LeRoux; one for Aza-Kra, as Mrs. Adrienne LeRoux. I pasted on the photographs and fed them into the machine that pressed the words, *"Photograph attached U. S. Consulate Paris, France"* into the paper, and then into the one that impressed the consular seal.

I signed them, and filled in the blanks on the inside covers, in the taxi on the way to the Israeli consulate. The afternoon was running out, and we had a lot to do.

We went to six foreign consulates, gassed the occupants, and got a visa stamp in each one. I had the devil's own time filling them out; I had to copy the scribbles I found in legitimate passports at each place and hope for the best. The Israeli one was surprisingly simple, but the Japanese was a horror.

We had dinner in our hotel room—steak for me, water and soybean paste, bought at a health-food store, for Aza-Kra. Just before we left for Le Bourget, I sent a cable to Eli Freeman: *Big story will have to wait spread this now all stockyard so-called epidemic and similar phenomena due one cause step on some body's toe to see what I mean.*

Shortly after seven o'clock we were aboard a flight bound for the Middle East.

And that was the fourth day, during which a number of things happened that I didn't have time to add to my list until later.

Commercial and amateur fishermen along the Atlantic seaboard, from Delaware Bay as far north as Portland, suffered violent attacks whose symptoms resembled those of asthma. Some—who had been using rods or poles rather than nets—complained also of sharp pains in the jaws and hard palate. Three deaths were reported.

The "epidemic" now covered roughly half of the continental United State's. All livestock shipments from the West had been cancelled, stockyards in the affected area, were full to bursting. The President had declared a national emergency.

Lobster had disappeared completely from east-coast menus.

One Robert James Dahl, described as the owner and publisher of a Middle Western newspaper, was being sought by the Defense Department and the FBI in connection with the disappearance of certain classified documents.

The next day, the fifth, was Saturday. At two in the morning on a Sabbath, Tel Aviv seemed as dead as Angkor. We had four hours there, between planes; we could have spent them in the airport waiting room, but I was wakeful and I wanted to talk to Aza-Kra. There was one ancient taxi at the airport; I had the driver take us into the town and leave us there, down in the harbor section, until plane time...

We sat on a bench behind the sea wall and watched the moonlight on the Mediterranean. Parallel banks of faintly silvered clouds arched over us to northward; the air was fresh and cool.

After awhile I said, "You know that I'm only playing this your way for one reason. As far as the rest of it goes, the more I think about it the less I like it."

"Why?"

"A dozen reasons. The biological angle, for one. I don't like violence, I don't like war, but it doesn't matter what I like. They're biologically necessary, they eliminate the unfit."

"Do you say that only the unfit are killed in wars?"

"That isn't what I mean. In modern war the contest isn't between individuals; it's between whole populations. Nations, and groups of nations. It's a cruel, senseless, wasteful business, and when you're in the middle of it it's hard to see any good at all in it, but it works—the survivors *survive*, and that's the only test there is."

"Our biologists do not take this view." He added, "Neither do yours."

I said, "How's that?"

"Your biologists agree with ours that war is not biological. It is social. When so many are killed, no stock improves. All suffer. It is as you yourself say, the contest is between nations. But their wars kill men."

I said, "All right, I concede that one. But we're not the only kind of animal on this planet, and we didn't get to be the dominant species without fighting. What are we supposed to do if we run into a hungry lion—argue with him?"

"In a few weeks there will be no more lions."

I stared at him. "This affects lions, too? Tigers, elephants, everything?"

"Everything of sufficient brain. Roughly, everything above the level of your insects."

"But I understood you to say that the catalyst-that it took a different catalyst for each species."

"No. All those with spines and warm blood have the same ancestors. Your snakes may perhaps need a different catalyst, and I believe you have some primitive sea creatures which kill, but they are not important."

I said, "My God." I thought of lions, wolves, coyotes, housecats, lying dead beside their prey. Eagles, hawks and owls tumbling out of the sky. Ferrets, stoats, weasels..."

The world a big garden, for protected children.

My fists clenched. "But this is a million times worse than I had any idea. It's insane. You're upsetting the whole natural balance, you're knocking it crossways. Just for a start, what the hell are we going to do about rats and mice? That's—" I choked on my tongue. There were too many images in my mind to put any of them into words. Rats like a tidal wave, filling a street from wall to wall. Deer swarming out of the forests. The sky blackening with crows, sparrows, jays...

"It will be difficult for some years," Aza-Kra said. "Perhaps even as difficult as you now think. But you say that to fight for survival is good. Is it not better to fight against other species than among yourselves?"

"Fight?" I said. "What have you left us to fight with? How many rats can a man kill before he drops dead from shock?"

"It is possible to kill without causing pain or shock... You would have thought of this, although it is a new idea for you. Even your killing of animals for food can continue. We do not ask you to become as old as we are in a day. Only to put behind you your cruelty which has no purpose."

He had answered me, as always; and as always, the answer was two-edged. It was possible to kill painlessly, yes. And the only weapon Aza-Kra had brought to Earth, apparently, was an anesthetic gas...

We landed at Srinagar, in the Vale of Kashmir, at high noon: a sea of white light under a molten-metal sky.

Crossing the field, I saw a group of white-turbaned figures standing at the gate. I squinted at them through the glare; heatwaves made them jump and waver, but in a moment I was sure. They were bush-bearded Sikh policemen, and there were eight of them.

I pressed Aza-Kra's arm sharply and held my breath.

A moment later we picked our way through the sprawled line of passengers to the huddle of bodies at the gate. The passport examiner, a slender Hindu, lay a yard from the Sikhs. I plucked a sheet of paper out of his hand.

Sure enough, it was a list of the serial numbers of the passports we had stolen from the Paris consulate.

Bad luck. It was only six-thirty in Paris now, and on a Saturday morning at that; we should have had at least six hours more. But something could have gone wrong at any one of the seven consulates—an after-hours appointment, or a worried wife, say. After that the whole thing would have unraveled.

"How much did you give them this time?" I asked.

"As before. Twenty hours."

"All right, good. Let's go."

He had overshot his range a little: all four of the hack-drivers waiting outside the airport building were snoring over their wheels. I dumped the skinniest one in the back seat with Aza-Kra and took over.

Not for the first time, it occurred to me that without me or somebody just like me Aza-Kra would be helpless. It wasn't just a matter of getting out of Chillicothe; he couldn't drive a car or fly a plane, he couldn't pass for human by himself; he couldn't speak without giving himself away. Free, with no broken bones, he could probably escape recapture indefinitely; but if he wanted to go anywhere he would have to walk.

And not for the first time, I tried to see into a history book that hadn't been written yet. My name was there, that much was certain, providing there was going to be any history to write. But was it a name like Blondel...or did it sound more like Vidkun Quisling?

We had to go south; there was nothing in any other direction but the highest mountains in the world. We didn't have Pakistan visas, so Lahore and Amritsar, the obvious first choices, were out. The best we could do was Chamba, about two hundred-rail miles southeast on the Srinagar-New Delhi line. It wasn't on the principal air routes but we could get a plane there to Saharanpur, which was.

There was an express leaving in half an hour, and we took it. I bought an English-language newspaper at the station and read it backwards and forwards for four hours; Aza-Kra spent the time apparently asleep, with his cone, hidden by the black hat, tilted out the window.

The "epidemic" had spread to five Western states, plus Quebec, Ontario and Manitoba, and parts of Mexico and Cuba plus England and France, I knew, but there was nothing about that in my Indian paper; too early.

In Chamba I bought the most powerful battery-operated portable radio I could find; I wished I had thought of it sooner. I checked with the airport: there was a flight leaving Saharanpur for Port Blair at eight o'clock.

Port Blair, in the Andamans, is Indian Territory; we wouldn't need to show our passports. What we were going to do after that was another question.

I could have raided another set of consulates, but I knew it would be asking for trouble. Once was bad enough; twice, and when we tried it a third time—as we would have to, unless I found some other answer—I was willing to bet we would find them laying for us, with gas masks and riot guns.

Somehow, in the few hours we were to spend at Port Blair, I had to get those serial numbers altered by an expert.

We had been walking the black, narrow dockside streets for two hours when Aza-Kra suddenly stopped.

"Something?"

"Wait," he said. "...Yes. This is the man you are looking for. He is a professional forger. His name is George Wheelwright. He can do it, but I do not know whether he will. He is a very timid and suspicious man."

"All right. In here?"

"Yes."

We went up a narrow unlighted stairway, choked with a kitchen midden of smells, curry predominating. At the second floor landing Aza-Kra pointed to a door. I knocked.

Scufflings behind the door. A low voice: "Who's that?"

"A friend. Let us in, Wheelwright."

The door cracked open and yellow light spilled out; I saw the outline of a head and the faint gleam of a bulbous eye. "What d'yer want?"

"Want you to do a job for me, Wheelwright. Don't keep us talking here in the hall."

The door opened wider and I squeezed through into a cramped, untidy box of a kitchen. A faded cloth covered the doorway to the next room.

Wheelwright glanced at Aza-Kra and then stared hard at me; he was a little chicken-breasted wisp of a man, dressed in dungarees and a striped polo shirt. "Who sent yer?"

"You wouldn't know the name. A friend of mine in Calcutta." I took out the passports. "Can you fix-these?"

He looked at them carefully, taking his time. "What's wrong with 'em?"

"Nothing but the serial numbers."

"What's wrong with *them?*"

"They're on a list."

He laughed, a short, meaningless bark.

I said, "Well?"

"Who'd yer say yer friend in Calcutter was?"

"I haven't got any friend in Calcutta. Never mind how I knew about you. Will you do the job or won't you?"

He handed the passports back and moved toward the door. "Mister, I haven't got the time to fool with yer. Perhaps yer having me on, or perhaps yer've made an honest mistake. There's another Wheelwright over on the north side of town. You try him." He opened the door. "Good night, both."

I pushed it shut again and reached for him, but he was a yard away in one jump, like a rabbit. He stood beside the table, arms hanging, and stared at me with a vague smile.

I said, "I haven't got time to play games. I'll pay you five hundred American dollars to alter these passports"—I tossed them onto the table—"or else I'll beat the living tar out of you." I took a step toward him.

I never saw a man move faster: he had the drawer open and the gun out and aimed before I finished that step. But the muzzle trembled slightly. "No nearer," he said hoarsely.

I thought, *Five minutes*, and held my breath.

When he slumped, I picked up the revolver. Then I lifted him—he weighed about ninety pounds—propped him in a chair behind the table, and waited.

In a few minutes he raised his bead and goggled at me dazedly. "How'd yer do that?" he whispered.

I put the money on the table beside the passports. "Start," I said.

He stared at it, then at me. His thin lips tightened, "Go ter blazes," he said.

I stepped around the table and cuffed him backhand, I felt the blow on my own face, hard and stinging, but I did it again, I kept it up. It wasn't pleasant; I was feeling not only the blows themselves, but Wheelwright's emotional responses, the shame and wretchedness and anger, and the queasy writhing fear: Wheelwright couldn't bear pain.

At that, he beat me. When I stopped, sickened and dizzy, and said as roughly as I could, "Had enough, Wheelwright?" he answered, "Not if yer was ter kill me, yer bloody barstid."

His voice trembled, and his face was streaked with tears, but he meant it. He thought I was a government agent, trying to bully him into signing his own prison sentence, and rather than let me do it he would take any amount of punishment; prison was the one thing he feared more than physical pain.

I looked at Aza-Kra. His neck-spines were erect and quivering; I could see the tips of them at the edges of the veil. Then inspiration hit me.

I pulled him forward where the little man could see him, and lifted the veil. The feathery spines stood out clearly on either side of the corpse-white mask.

"I won't touch you again," I said. "But look at this. Can you see?"

His eyes widened; he scrubbed them with the palms of his hands and looked again.

"And this," I said, I pulled at Aza-Kra's forearm and the clawed blue-gray hand came out of the muff.

Wheelwright's eyes bulged. He flattened himself against the back of the chair.

"Now," I said, "six hundred dollars—or I'll take this mask off and show you what's behind it."

He clenched his eyes shut. His face had gone yellowish-pale; his nostrils were white.

"Get it out of here," he said faintly.

He didn't move until Aza-Kra had disappeared behind the curtain into the other room. Then, without a word, he poured and drank half a tumblerful of whiskey, switched on a gooseneck lamp, produced bottles, pens and brushes from the table drawer, and went to work. He bleached away the first and last digits of both serial numbers, then painted over the areas with a thin wash of color that matched the blue tint of the paper. With a jeweler's loupe in his eye, he restored the obliterated tiny letters of the background design; finally, still using the loupe, he drew the new digits in black. From first to last, it took him thirty minutes; and his hands didn't begin to tremble until he was done.

CHAPTER FIVE

The sixth day was two days—because we left Otaru at 3:30 p.m. Sunday and arrived at Honolulu at 11:30 p.m. Saturday. We had lost four and a half-hours in traversing sixty-two degrees of longitude—but we'd also gained a day by crossing the International Date Line from west to east.

On the sixth day, then, which was two days, the following things happened and were duly reported:

Be Done By As Ye Do was the title of some thousands of sermons and, by count more than seven hundred front page newspaper editorials from Newfoundland to Oaxaca. My cable to Freeman had come a little late; the *Herald-Star's* announcement was lost in the ruck.

Following this, a wave of millennial enthusiasm swept the continent; Christians and Jews everywhere feasted, fasted, prayed and in other ways celebrated the imminent Second (or First) Coming of Christ. Evangelistic and fundamentalist sects garnered souls by the million.

Members of the Apostolic Overcoming Holy Church of God, the Pentecostal Fire Baptized Holiness Church and numerous other groups gave away most or all of their worldly possessions. Others were more practical. The Seventh Day Adventists, who are vegetarians, pooled capital and began an enormous expansion of their meatless-food factories, dairies and other enterprises.

Delegates to a World Synod of Christian Churches began arriving at a tent city near Smith Center, Kansas, late Saturday night. Trouble developed almost immediately between the Brethren Church of God (Reformed Dunkers) and the Two-Seed-in-the-Spirit Predestinarian Baptists—later spreading to a schism which led to the establishment of two rump synods, one at Lebanon and the other at Athol.

Five hundred Doukhobors stripped themselves mother-naked, burned their homes, and marched on Vancouver.

Roman Catholics in most places celebrated the Feast of the Transfiguration as usual, awaiting advice from Rome.

Riot's broke out in Chicago, Detroit, New Orleans, Philadelphia and New York. In each case the original disturbances were brief, but were followed by protracted vandalism and looting which local police, state police, and even National Guard units were unable to cheek. By midnight Sunday property damage was estimated at more than twenty million dollars. The casualty list was fantastically high. So was the proportion of police and National Guard casualties—exactly fifty per cent of the total.

In the British Isles, Western Europe and Scandinavia the early symptoms of the Western hemisphere's disaster were beginning to appear: the stricken slaughterers and fishermen, the unease in prisons, the freaks of violence.

An unprecedented number of political refugees turned up on the East-German side of the Burnt Corridor early Saturday morning.

Late the same day, a clash between Sikh and Moslem guards on the India-Pakistan border near Sialkot resulted in the annihilation of both parties.

And on Sunday it hit the fighting in Indo-China.

Allied and Communist units, engaging at sixty points along the eight-hundred-mile front, fell back with the heaviest casualties of the war.

Red bombers launched a successful daylight attack on Luangprabang: successful, that is, except that nineteen out of twenty planes crashed outside the city or fell into the Nam Ou.

Forty Allied bombers took off on sorties to Yen-bay, Hanoi and Nam-dinh. None returned.

Nobody knew it yet, but the war was over.

Still other things happened but were not recorded by the press:

A man in Arizona, a horse gelder by profession, gave up his business and moved out of the county, alleging ill health.

So did a dentist in Tacoma, and another in Galveston.

In Breslau an official of the People's Police resigned his position with the same excuse; and one in Buda; and one in Pest.

A conservative Tajik tribesman of Indarab discovering that his new wife had been unfaithful, attempted to deal with her in the traditional manner, but desisted when a critical observer would have said he had hardly begun; nor did this act of compassion bring him any relief.

And outside the town of Otaru, just two hundred and, fifty miles across the Sea of Japan from the eastern shore of the Russian Socialist Federated Soviet Republic, Aza-Kra used his anesthetic gas again—on me.

I had been bone-tired when we left Port Blair shortly before midnight, but I hadn't slept all the long, dark droning way to Manila; or from there to Tokyo, with the sun rising half an hour after we cleared the Philippines and slowly turning the globe underneath us to a white disk of fire; or from Tokyo north again to Otaru, bleak and windy and smelling of brine.

In all that time, I hadn't been able to forget Wheelwright except for half an hour toward the end, when I picked up an English-language broadcast from Tokyo and heard the news from the States.

The first time you burn yourself playing with matches, the chances are that if the blisters aren't too bad, you get over it fast enough; you forget about it. But the second time, it's likely to sink in.

Wheelwright was my second time; Wheelwright finished me.

It's more than painful, it's more than frightening, to cause another living creature pain and feel what he feels. It tears you apart. It makes you the victor and the victim, and neither half of that is bearable.

It makes you love what you destroy—as you love yourself and it makes you hate yourself as your victim hates you.

That isn't all. I had felt Wheelwright's self-loathing as his body cringed and the tears spilled out of his eyes, the helpless gut-twisting shame that was as bad as the fear; and that burden was on me too.

Wheelwright was talented. That was his achievement; he had found it in himself and developed it and trained himself to use it. Wheelwright had courage. That was his own. But who had made Wheelwright afraid? And who had taught him that the world was his enemy?

You, and I, and every other human being on the planet, and all our two-legged ancestors before us. Because we had settled for too little. Because not more than a handful of us, out of all the crawling billions, had ever had the will to break the chain of blows, from father to daughter to son, generation after generation.

So there was Wheelwright; that was what we had made out of man: the artistry and the courage compressed to a needle-thin, needle-hard core inside him, and that only because we hadn't been able to destroy it altogether; the rest of him self-hatred, and suspicion, and resentment, and fear.

But after breakfast in Tokyo, it began to seem a little more likely that some kind of a case could be made for the continued existence of the human race. And after that it was natural to think about lions and about the rioting that was going on in America.

For all his moral nicety, Aza-Kra had no trouble in justifying the painful extinction of carnivores. From his point of view, they were better off dead. It was regrettable, of course, but...

But, *sub specie aeternitatis,* was a man much different from a lion?

It was a commonplace that no other animal killed on so grand a scale as man. The problem had never come up before: could we live without killing?

I was standing with Aza-Kra at the top of a little hill that overlooked the coast road and the bay. The bus that had brought us there was dwindling, a white speck in a cloud of dust, down the highway toward Cape Kamui.

Aza-Kra sat on a stone, his third leg grotesquely bulging the skirt of his coat. His head bent forward, as if the old woman he was pretending to be had fallen asleep, chin on massive chest; the conical hat pointed out to sea.

I said, "This is the time of crisis you were talking about, for America."

"Yes. It begins now."

"When does it end? Let's talk about this a little more. This justice. Crimes of violence—all right. They punish themselves, and before long they'll prevent themselves, automatically. What about crimes of property? A man steals my wallet and runs. Or he smashes a window and takes what he wants. Who's going to stop him?"

He didn't answer for a moment; when he did the words came slowly and the pronunciation was bad, as if he were too weary to attend to it. "The wallet can be chained to your clothing. The window can be made of glass that does not break."

I said impatiently, "You know that's not what I mean, I'm talking about the problem as it affects everybody. We solve it by policemen and courts and prisons. What do we do instead?"

"I am sorry that I did not understand you. Give me a moment..."

I waited.

"In your Middle Ages, when a man was insane, what did you do?"

I thought of Bedlam, and of creatures with matted hair chained to rooftops.

He didn't wait for me to speak. "Yes. And now, you are more wise?"

"A little."

"Yes. And in the beginning of your Industrial Revolution, when a factory stopped and men had no work, what was done?"

"They starved."

"And now?"

"There are relief organizations. We try to keep them alive until they can get work."

"If a man steals what he does not need," Aza-Kra said, "is he not sick? If a man steals what he must have to live, can you blame him?"

Socrates, in an onyx-trimmed dress, three-legged on a stone.

Finally I said, "It's easy enough to make us look foolish, but we have made some progress in the last two thousand years. Now you want us to go the rest of the way overnight. It's impossible; we haven't got time enough."

"You will have more time now." His voice was very faint. "Killing wastes much time... Forgive me, now I must sleep."

His head dropped even farther forward. I watched for awhile to see if he would topple over, but of course he was too solidly based. A tripod. I sat down beside him, feeling my own fatigue drag at my body, envying him his rest; but I couldn't sleep.

There was really no point in arguing with him, I told myself; he was too good for me. I was a savage splitting logic with a missionary. He knew more than I did; probably he was more intelligent. And the central question, the only one that mattered, couldn't be answered the way I was going at it.

Aza-Kra himself was the key, not the doctrine of non-violence, not the psychology of crime.

If he was telling the truth about himself and the civilization he came from, I had nothing to worry about.

If he wasn't, then I should have left him in Chillicothe or killed him in Paris; and if I could kill him now, that was what I should do.

And I didn't know. After all this time, I still didn't know.

I saw the bus come back down the road and disappear towards Otaru. After a long time, I saw it heading out again. When it came back from the cape the second time, I woke Aza-Kra and we slogged down the steep path to the roadside. I waved as the bus came nearer; it slowed and rattled to a halt a few yards beyond us.

Passengers heads popped out of the windows to watch us as we walked toward the door. Most of them were Japanese, but I saw one Caucasian, leaning with both arms out the window. I saw his features clearly, narrow pale nose and lips, blue eyes, behind rimless glasses; sunlight glinting on sparse yellow hair. And then I saw the flat dusty road coming up to meet me.

I was lying face-up on a hard sandy slope; when I opened my eyes I saw the sky and a few blades of tough, dry grass. The first thought that came into my head was, *Now I know. Now I've had it.*

I sat up. And a buzzing voice said, "Hold your breath!"

Turning, I saw a body sprawled on the slope just below me. It was the yellow-haired man. Beyond him squatted the gray form of Aza-Kra.

"All right," he said.

I let my breath out. "What—?"

He showed me a brown metal ovoid, cross-hatched with fragmentation grooves. A grenade.

"He was about to arm it. There was no time to warn you. I knew you would wish to see for yourself."

I looked around dazedly. Thirty feet above, the slope ended in a clean-cut line against the sky; beyond it was a short, narrow white stripe that I recognized as the top of the bus, still parked at the side of the road.

"We have ten minutes more before the others awaken."

I went through the man's pockets. I found a handful of change, a wallet with nothing in it but a few yen notes, and a folded slip of glossy white paper. That was all.

I unfolded the paper, but I knew what it was even before I saw the small teleprinted photograph on its inner side. It was a copy of my passport picture the one on the genuine document, not the bogus one I had made in Paris.

On the way back, my hands began shaking. It got so bad that I had to put them between my thighs and squeeze hard; and then the shaking spread to my legs and arms and jaw. My forehead was cold and there was a football-sized ache in my belly, expanding to a white pain every time we hit a bump. The whole bus seemed to be tilting ponderously over to the right, farther and farther but never falling down.

Later, when I had had a cup of coffee and two cigarettes in the terminal lunch room, I got one of the most powerful irrational impulses I've ever known: I wanted to take the next bus back to that spot on the coast road, walk down the slope to where the yellow-haired man was, and kick his skull to flinders.

If we were lucky, the yellow haired man might have been the only one in Otaru who knew we were here. The only way to find out was to go on to the airport and take a chance; either way, we had to get out of Japan. But it didn't end there. Even if they didn't know where we were now, they knew all the stops on our itinerary; they knew which visas we had. Maybe Aza-Kra would be able to gas the next one before he killed us, and then again maybe not.

I thought about Frisbee and Parst and the President—damning them all impartially—and my anger grew. By now, I realized suddenly, they must have understood that we were responsible for what was happening. They would have been energetically apportioning the blame for the last few days; probably Parst had already been court-martialed.

Once that was settled, there would be two things they could do next. They could publish the truth, admit their own responsibility, and warn the world. Or they could destroy all the evidence and keep silent. If the world went to hell in a bucket, at least they wouldn't be blamed for it... Providing I was dead. Not much choice.

After another minute I got up and Aza-Kra followed me out to a taxi. We stopped at the nearest telegraph office and I sent a cable to Frisbee in Washington: HAVE SENT FULL ACCOUNT CHILLICOTHE TO TRUSTWORTHY PERSON WITH INSTRUCTIONS PUBLISH EVENT MY DEATH OR DISAPPEARANCE. CALL OFF YOUR DOGS.

It was childish, but apparently it worked. Not only did we have no trouble at the Otaru airport—the yellow-haired man, as I'd hoped, must have been working alone—but nobody bothered us at Honolulu or Asuncion.

Just the same, the mood of depression and nervousness that settled on me that day didn't lift; it grew steadily worse. Fourteen hours' sleep in Asuncion didn't mend it; Monday's reports of panics and bank failures in North America intensified it, but that was incidental.

And when I slept, I had nightmares: dreams of stifling-dark jungles, full of things with teeth.

We spent twenty-four hours in Asuncion, while Aza-Kra pumped out enough catalyst to blanket South America's seven million square miles—a territory almost as big as the sprawling monster of Soviet Eurasia.

After that we flew to Capetown—and that was it. We were finished.

We had spiraled around the globe, from the United States to England, to France, to Israel, to India, to Japan, to Paraguay, to the Union of South Africa, trailing an expanding invisible cloud behind us. Now the trade winds were carrying it eastward from the Atlantic, south from the Mediterranean, north from the Indian Ocean, west from the Atlantic.

Frigate birds and locusts, men in tramp steamers and men in jet planes would carry it farther. In a week it would have reached all the places we had missed: Australia, Micronesia, the islands of the South Pacific, the Poles.

That left the lunar bases and the orbital stations. Ours and Theirs. But they had to be supplied from Earth; the infection would come to them in rockets.

For better or worse, we had what we had always said we wanted. Ahimsa. The Age of Reason. The Kingdom of God.

And I still didn't know whether I was Judas, or the little Dutch boy with his finger in the dike.

I didn't find out until three weeks later.

We stayed on in Capetown, resting and waiting. Listening to the radio and reading newspapers kept me occupied a good part of the time. When restlessness drove me out of doors, I wandered aimlessly in the business section, or went down to the harbor and spent hours staring out past the castle and the breakwater.

But my chief occupation, the thing that obsessed me now, was the study of Aza-Kra.

He seemed very tired. His skin was turning dry and rough, more gray than blue; his eyes were blue-threaded and more opaque looking than ever. He slept a great deal and moved little. The soybean paste I was able to get for him gave him insufficient nourishment; vitamins and minerals were lacking.

I asked him why he didn't make what he needed in his air machine. He said that some few of the compounds could be inhaled, and he was making those; that he had had another transmuter, for food-manufacture, but that it had been taken from him; and that he would be all right; he would last until his friends came.

He didn't know when that would be; or he wouldn't tell me.

His speech was slower and his diction more slurred every day. It was obviously difficult for him to talk; but I goaded him, I nagged him, I would not let him alone. I spent days on one topic, left it, came back to it and asked the same questions over. I made copious notes of what he said and the way he said it.

I wanted to learn to read the signs of his emotions; or failing that, to catch him in a lie.

A dozen times I thought I had trapped him into a contradiction, and each time, wearily, patiently, he explained what I had misunderstood. As for his emotions, they had only one visible sign that I was able to discover: the stiffening and trembling of his neck-spines.

Gestures of emotion are arbitrary. There are human tribes whose members never smile. There are others who smile when they are angry. Cf. Dodgson's Cheshire Cat.

He was doing it more and more often as the time went by; but what did it mean?

Anger? Resentment? Annoyance? *Amusement?*

The riots in the United States ended on the 9th and 10th when interfaith committees toured each city in loudspeaker trucks. Others began elsewhere.

Business was at a standstill in most larger cities. Galveston, Nashville and Birmingham joined in celebrating Hallelujah Week: dancing in the streets, bonfires day and night, every church and every bar roaring wide open.

Russia's delegate to the United Nations, who had been larding his speeches with mock-sympathetic references to the Western nations' difficulties, arose on the 9th and delivered a furious three-hour tirade accusing the entire non-Communist world of cowardly cryptofascistic biological warfare against the Soviet Union and the People's Republics of Europe and Asia.

The new staffs of the Federal penitentiaries in America, in office less than a week, followed their predecessors in mass resignations. The last official act of the wardens of Leavenworth, Terre Haute and Alcatraz was to report the "escape" of their entire prison populations.

Police officers in every major city were being frantically urged to remain on duty.

Queen Elizabeth, in a memorable speech, exhorted all citizens of the Empire to remain calm and meet whatever might come with dignity, fortitude and honor.

The Scots stole the Stone of Scone again.

Rioting and looting began in Paris, Marseilles, Barcelona, Milan, Amsterdam, Munich, Berlin.

The Pope was silent.

Turkey declared war on Syria and Iraq; peace was concluded a record three hours later.

On the 10th, Warsaw Radio announced the formation of a new Polish Provisional Government whose first and second acts had been, respectively, to abrogate all existing treaties with the Soviet Union and border states, and to petition the UN for restoration of the 1938 boundaries.

On the 11th East Germany, Austria, Czechoslovakia, Hungary, Rumania, Bulgaria, Latvia and Lithuania followed suit, with variations on the boundary question.

On the 12th, after a brief but by no means bloodless putsch, the Spanish Republic was reestablished; the British government fell once and the French government twice; and the Vatican issued a sharp protest against the ill treatment of priests and nuns by Spanish insurgents.

Not a shot had been fired in Indo-China since the morning of the 8th.

On the 13th the Karelo-Finnish S. S. R., the Estonian S.S.R., the Byelorussian S.S.R., the Ukrainian S.S.R., the Azerbaijan S.S.R., the Turkmen S.S.R. and the Uzbek S.S.R. declared their independence of the Soviet Union. A horde of men and women escaped or released from forced-labor camps, the so-called Slave Army, poured westward out of Siberia.

CHAPTER SIX

On the 14th, Zebulon, Georgia (pop. 312), Murfreesboro, Tennessee (pop. 11,190) and Orange, Texas (pop. 8,470) seceded from the Union.

That might have been funny, but on the 15th petitions for a secession referendum were wildly circulating in Tennessee, Arkansas, Louisiana and South Carolina. Early returns averaged 61% in favor.

On the 16th Texas: Oklahoma, Mississippi, Alabama, Kentucky, Virginia, Georgia and—incongruously—Rhode Island and Minnesota added themselves to the list. Separatist fever was rising in Quebec, New Brunswick, Newfoundland and Labrador. Across the Atlantic, Catalonia, Bavaria,

Moldavia, Sicily and Cyprus declared themselves independent states.

And that might have been hysteria. But that wasn't all.

Liquor stores and bars were sprouting like mushrooms in dry states. Ditto gambling halls, horse rooms, houses of prostitution, cockpits, burlesque theaters.

Moonshine whisky threatened for a few days to become the South's major industry, until standard-brand distillers cut their prices to meet the competition. Not a bottle of the new stocks of liquor carried a Federal tax stamp.

Mexican citizens were walking across the border into Arizona and New Mexico, swimming into Texas. The first shipload of Chinese arrived in San Francisco on the 16th.

Meat prices had increased by an average of 60% for every day since the new control and rationing law took effect. By the 16th, round steak was selling for $10.80 a pound.

Resignations of public officials were no longer news; a headline in the Portland *Oregonian* for August 15th read: WILL STAY AT DESK, SAYS GOVERNOR.

It hit me hard.

But when I thought about it, it was obvious enough; it was such an elementary thing that ordinarily you never noticed it—that all governments, not just tyrannies, but *all* governments were based on violence, as currency was based on metal. You might go for months or years without seeing a silver dollar or a policeman ; but the dollar and the policeman had to be there.

The whole elaborate structure, the work of a thousand years, was coming down. The value of a dollar is established by a promise to pay; the effectiveness of a law, by a threat to punish.

Even if there were enough jailers left, how could you put a man in jail if he had ten or twenty friends who didn't want him to go?

How many people were going to pay their income taxes next year, even if there was a government left to pay them to?

And who was going to stop the landless people from spilling over into the nations that had land to spare?

Aza-Kra said, "These things are not necessary to do."

I turned around and looked at him. He had been lying motionless for more than an hour in the hammock I had rigged for him at the end of the room; I had thought he was asleep.

It was raining outside. Dim, colorless light came through the slotted window blinds and striped his body like a melted barber pole. Caught in one of the bars of light, the tips of two quivering neck-spines glowed in faint filigree against the shadow.

"All right," I said. "Explain this one away, I'd d like to hear you. Tell me why we don't need governments any more."

"The governments you have now—the governments of nations—they are not made for use. They exist to fight other nations."

"That's not true."

"It is true. Think. Of the money your government spends in a year, how much is for war and how much for use?"

"About sixty per cent for war. But that doesn't—"

"Please. This is sixty percent now, when you have only a small war. When you have a large war, how much then?"

"Ninety percent. Maybe more, but that hasn't got anything to do with it. In peace or wartime there are things a national government does that can't be done by anybody else. Now ask me for instance, what."

"Yes. I ask this."

"For instance, keeping an industrial country from being dragged down to coolie level by unrestricted immigration."

"You think it is better for those who have much to keep apart from those who have little, and give no help?"

"In principle, no, but it isn't just that easy. What good does it do the starving Asiatics if we turn America into another piece of Asia and starve along with them?"

He looked at me unwinkingly.

"What good has it done to keep apart?"

I opened my mouth, and shut it again. Last time it had been Japan, an island chain a little smaller than California. In the next one, half the world would have been against us.

"The problem is not easy, it is very difficult. But to solve it by helping is possible. To solve it by doing nothing is not possible."

"Harbors," I said softly. "Shipping. Soil conservation. Communications. Flood control."

"You do not believe these things can be done if there are no nations?"

"No. We haven't got time enough to pick up all the pieces. It's a hell of a lot easier to knock things apart than to put them together again."

"Your people have done things more difficult than this. You do not believe now, but you will see it done."

After a moment I said, "We're supposed to become a member of your galactic union now. Now that you've pulled our teeth. Who's going to build the ships?"

"Those who build them now."

I said, "Governments build them now."

"No. Men build ships. Men invent ships and design ships. Government builds nothing but more government."

I put my fists in my pockets and walked over to the window. Outside, a man went hurrying by in the rain, one hand at his hat-brim, the other at his chest. He didn't look around as he passed; his coffee-brown face was intent and impersonal, I watched him until he turned the corner, out of sight.

He had never heard of me, but his life would be changed by what I had done. His descendants would know my name; they would be bored by it in school, or their mothers would frighten them with it after dark...

Aza-Kra said, "To talk of these things is useless. If I would lie, I would not tell you that I lie. And if I would lie about these things, I would lie well; you would not find the truth by questions. You must wait. Soon you will know."

I looked at him. "When your friends come."

"Yes," he said.

And the feathery tips of his neck-spines delicately trembled.

They came on the last day of August—fifty great rotiform ships drifting down out of space. No radar spotted them; no planes or interceptor rockets went up to meet them. They followed the terminator around, landing at dawn: thirty in the Americas, twenty in Europe and Asia, five in Africa, one each in England, Scandinavia, Australia, New Zealand, New Guinea, the Philippines, Japan.

Each one was six hundred feet across, but they rested lightly on the ground. Where they landed on sloping land, slender curved supporting members came out of the doughnut-shaped rim, as dainty as insect's legs, and the fat lozenge of the hub lowered itself on the five fat spokes until it touched the earth.

Their doors opened.

In twenty-four days I had watched the nations of the Earth melt into shapelessness like sculptures molded of silicone putty. Armies, navies, air forces, police forces lost their cohesion first. In the beginning there were individual desertions, atoms escaping one at a time from the mass; later, when the pay failed to arrive, when there were no orders or else orders that could not be executed, men and women simply went home, orderly, without haste, in thousands.

Every useful item of equipment that could be carried or driven or flown went with them. Tractors, trucks, jeeps, bulldozers gladdened the hearts of farmers from Keokuk to Kweiyang. Bombers, small boats, even destroyers and battleships were in service as commercial transports. Quartermasters' stores were carried away piecemeal or in ton lots. Guns and ammunition rusted undisturbed.

Stock markets crashed. Banks failed. Treasuries failed. National governments broke down into states, provinces, cantons. In the United States, the President resigned his office on the 18th and left the White House, whose every window had been broken and whose lawn was newly landscaped with eggshells and orange rind. The Vice-President resigned the next day, leaving the Presidency, in theory, to the Speaker of the House; but the Speaker was at home on his Arkansas farm; Congress had adjourned on the 17th.

Everywhere it was the same. The new Governments of Asia and Eastern Europe, of Spain and Portugal and Argentina and Iran, died stillborn.

The Moon colonies had been evacuated; work had stopped on the Mars rocket. The men on duty in the orbital stations, after an anxious week, had reached an agreement for mutual disarmament and had come down to Earth.

Seven industries out of ten had closed down. The dollar was worth half a penny, the pound sterling a little more; the rouble, the Reichsmark, the franc, the sen, the yen, the rupee were waste paper.

The great cities were nine-tenths deserted, gutted by fires, the homes of looters, rats and roaches.

Even the local governments, the states, the cantons, the counties, the very townships, were too fragile to stand. All the arbitrary lines on the map had lost their meaning.

You could not say any more, "Japan will—" or "India is moving toward—" It was startling to realize that; to have to think of a sprawling, amorphous, unfathomable mass of infinitely varied human beings instead of a single inclusive symbol. It made you wonder if the symbol had ever had any connection with reality at all: whether there had ever been such a thing as a nation.

Toward the end of the month, I thought I saw a flicker of hope. The problem of famine was being attacked vigorously and efficiently by the Red Cross, the Salvation Army, and thousands of local volunteer groups: they commandeered fleets of trucks, emptied warehouses with a calm disregard of legality, and distributed the food where it was most needed. It was not enough –too much food had been destroyed and wasted by looters, too much had spoiled through neglect, and too much had been destroyed in the field by wandering, half-starved bands of the homeless—but it was a beginning; it was something.

Other groups were fighting the problem of these wolf packs, with equally encouraging results. Farmers were forming themselves into mutual-defense groups, "communities of force." Two men could take any property from one man of equal strength without violence, without the penalty of pain; but not from two men, or three men.

One district warned the next when a wolf pack was on the way, and how many to expect. When the pack converged on a field or a storehouse, men in equal or greater numbers were there to stand in the way. If the district could absorb, say, ten workers, that many of the pack were offered the option of staying; the rest had to move on. Gradually, the packs thinned.

In the same way, factories were able to protect themselves from theft, by an extension of the idea, even the money problem began to seem soluble. The old currency was all but worthless, and an individual's promise to pay in kind was no better as a medium of exchange; but promissory notes obligating whole communities could and did begin to circulate. They made an unwieldy currency, their range was limited, and they depreciated rapidly. But it was something; it was a beginning.

Then the wheel-ships came.

In every case but one, they were cautious. They landed in conspicuous positions, near a city or a village, and in the dawn light, before any man had come near them, oddly shaped things came out and hurriedly unloaded boxes and bales, hundreds, thousands, a staggering array. They setup sun-reflecting beacons; then the ships rose again and disappeared, and when the first men came hesitantly out to investigate, they found nothing but the beacon, the acre of carefully-stacked boxes, and the signs, in the language of the country, that said:

THIS FOOD IS SENT BY THE PEOPLES OF

OTHER WORLDS TO HELP YOU IN YOUR NEED.

ALL MEN ARE BROTHERS.

And a brave man would lift the top of a box; inside he would see other boxes, and in them oblong pale shapes wrapped in something transparent that was not cellophane. He would unwrap one, feel it, smell it, show it around, and finally taste it; and then his eyebrows would go up.

The color and the texture were unfamiliar, but the taste was unmistakable! Tortillas and beans! (Or taro; or rice with bean-sprouts; or stuffed-grape leaves; or herb omelette!)

The exception was the ship that landed outside Capetown, in an open field at the foot of Table Mountain.

Aza-Kra woke me at dawn. "They are here."

I mumbled at him and tried to turn over. He shook my shoulder again, buzzing excitedly to himself. "Please, they are here. We must hurry."

I lurched out of bed and stood swaying. "Your friends?" I said.

"Yes, yes." He was struggling into the black dress, pushing the peaked hat backwards onto his head. *"Hurry."*

I splashed cold water on my face, and got into my clothes. I pulled out the tap dresser drawer and looked at the two loaded, automatics. I couldn't decide, I couldn't figure out any way they would do me any good, but I didn't want to leave them behind. I stood there until my legs went numb before I could make up my mind to take them anyhow, and the hell with it.

There were no taxis, of course. We walked for three blocks along the deserted streets until we saw a battered sedan nose into view in the intersection ahead, moving cautiously around the heaps of litter.

"Hold your breath!"

The car moved on out of sight.

We found it around the corner, up on the sidewalk with the front fender jammed against a railing. There were two men and a woman in it, Europeans.

"Which way?"

"Left. To the mountain."

When we got to the outskirts and the buildings began to thin out, I saw it up ahead, a huge silvery-metal shelf jutting out impossibly from the slope. I began to tremble. *They'll cut me up and put me in a jar, I thought. Now is the time to stop, if I'm going to.*

But I kept going. Where the road veered away from the field and went curving on up the mountain the other way. I stopped and we got out. I saw dark shapes and movements under that huge gleaming bulk. We stepped over a broken fence and started across the dry uneven clods in the half-light.

Light sprang out: a soft, pearl-gray shimmer that didn't dazzle the eye although it was aimed straight towards us, marking the way. I heard a shrill wordless buzzing, and above that an explosion of chirping, and under them both a confusion of other sounds, humming, droning, clattering. I saw a half-dozen nightmare shapes bounding forward.

Two of them were like Aza-Kra; two more were squat things with huge humped shells on top, like tortoise-shells the size of a card table, with six long stump-ended legs underneath, and a tangle of eyes, tentacles, and small wriggly things peeping out in front; one, the tallest, had a long sharp-spined column of a body rising from a thick base and four startlingly human legs, and surmounted by four long whiplike tentacles and a smooth oval head; the sixth looked at first glance like an unholy cross between a grasshopper and a newt. He came in twenty-foot bounds.

They crowded around Aza-Kra, humming, chirping, droning, buzzing, clattering. Their hands and tentacles went over him, caressingly; the newt-grasshopper thing hoisted him onto its back.

They paid no attention to me, and I stayed where I was, with my hands tight and sweating on the grips of my guns. Then I heard Aza-Kra speak, and the tallest one turned back to me.

It reeked: something like brine, something like wet fur, something rank and indescribable. It had two narrow red eyes in that smooth knob of a head. It put one of its tentacles on my shoulder, and I didn't see a mouth open anywhere, but a droning voice said, "Thank you for caring for him. Come now. We go to ship."

I pulled away instinctively, quivering, and my hands came out of my pockets, I heard a flat, echoing *crack* and a yell, and I saw a red wetness spring out across the smooth skull; I saw the thing topple and lie in the dirt, twitching.

I thought for an instant that I had done it, the shot, the yell and all. Then I heard another yell, behind me; I whirled around and heard a car grind into gear and saw it bouncing away down the road into town, lights off, a black moving shape on the dimness. I saw it veer wildly and slew into the fence at the first turn; I heard its tires popping as it went through and the muffled crash as it turned over.

Dead, I thought. But the next minute I saw two figures come erect beyond the overturned car and stagger toward the road. They disappeared around the turn, running.

I looked back at the others, bewildered. They weren't even looking that way; they were gathered around the body, lifting it, carrying it toward the ship.

The feeling—the black depression that had been getting stronger every day for three weeks—tightened down on me as if somebody had turned a screw, I gritted my teeth against it, and stood there wishing I were dead.

They were almost to the open hatch in the oval hub that hung under the rim when Aza-Kra detached himself from the group and walked slowly back to me. After a moment one of the others—a hump-shelled one—trundled along after him and waited a yard or two away.

"It is not your fault," said Aza-Kra. "We could have prevented it, but we were careless. We were so glad to meet that we did not take precautions. It is not your fault. Come to the ship."

The hump-shelled thing came up and squeaked something, and Aza-Kra sat on its back. The tentacles waved at me. It wheeled and started toward the hatchway. "Come," said Aza-Kra.

I followed them, too miserable to care what happened. We went down a corridor full of the sourceless pearl-gray light until a doorway suddenly appeared, somehow, and we went through that into a room where two tri-peds were waiting.

Aza-Kra climbed onto a stool, and one of the tri-peds began pressing two small instruments against various parts of his body; the other squirted something from a flexible canister into his mouth.

And as I stood there watching, between one breath and the next, the depression went away.

I felt like a man whose toothache has just stopped; I probed at my mind, gingerly, expecting to find that the feeling was still there, only hiding. But it wasn't. It was gone so completely that I couldn't even remember exactly what it had been like. I felt calm and relaxed—and safe.

I looked at Aza-Kra. He was breathing easily; his eyes looked clearer then they had a moment before, and it seemed to me that his skin was glossier. The feathery neck-spines hung in relaxed, graceful curves.

...It was all true, then. It had to be. If they had been conquerors, the automatic death of the man who had killed one of their number, just now, wouldn't have been enough. An occupying army can never be satisfied with an eye for an eye. There must be revenge.

But they hadn't done anything; they hadn't even used the gas. They'd seen that the others in the car were running away, that the danger was over, and that ended it. The only emotions they had shown, as far as I could tell, were concern and regret—

Except that, I remembered now, I had seen two of the tripeds clearly when I turned back to look at them gathering around the body: Aza-Kra and another one. And their neck-spines had been stiff...

Suddenly I knew the answer.

Aza-Kra came from a world where violence and cruelty didn't exist. To him, the Earth was a jungle—and I was one of its carnivores.

I knew, now, why I had felt the way I had for the last three weeks, and why the feeling had stopped a few minutes ago. My hostility toward him had been partly responsible for his fear, and so I had picked up an echo of it. Undirected fear is, by definition, anxiety, depression, uneasiness—the psychologists' *Angst*. It had stopped because Aza-Kra no longer had to depend on me; he was with his own people again; he was safe.

I knew the reason for my nightmares.

I knew why, time and again when I had expected Aza-Kra to be reading my mind, I had found that he wasn't. He did it only when he had to; it was too painful.

And one thing more:

I knew that when the true history of this time came to be written, I needn't worry about my place in it. My name would be there, all right, but nobody would remember it once he had shut the book.

Nobody would use my name as an insulting epithet, and nobody would carve it on the bases of any statues, either.

I wasn't the hero of the story.

It was Aza-Kra who had come down alone to a planet so deadly that no one else would risk his life on it until he had softened it up. It was Aza-Kra who had lived for nearly a month with a suspicious, irrational, combative, uncivilized flesh-eater. It was Aza-Kra who had used me, every step of the way—used my provincial loyalties and my self-interest and my prejudices.

He had done all that, weary, tortured, half-starved...and he'd been scared to death the whole time.

We made two stops up the coast and then moved into Algeria and the Sudan: landing, unloading, taking off again, following the dawn line. The other ships, Aza-Kra explained, would keep on circling the planet until enough food had been distributed to prevent any starvation until the next harvests. This one was going only as far as the middle of the North American continent to drop me off. Then it was going to take Aza-Kra home.

I watched what happened after we left each place in a vision device they had. In some places there was more hesitation than in others, but in the end they always took the food: in jeeploads, by pack train, in baskets balanced on their heads.

Some of the repeaters worried me. I said, "How do you know it'll get distributed to everybody who needs it?"

I might have known the answer: "They will distribute it. No man can let his neighbor starve while he has plenty."

The famine relief was all they had come for, this time. Later, when we had got through the crisis, they would come back; and by that time, remembering the food, people would be more inclined to take them on their merits instead of shuddering because they had too many eyes or fingers. They would help us when we needed it, they would show us the way up the ladder, but we would have to do the work ourselves.

He asked me not to publish the story of Chillicothe and the month we had spent together. "Later, when it will hurt no one, you can explain. Now there is no need to make anyone ashamed; not even the officials of your government. It was not their fault; they did not make the planet as it was." So there went even that two-bit chance at immortality.

It was still dawn when we landed on the bluff across the river from my home; sky and land and water were all the same depth less cool gray, except for the hairline of scarlet in the east. Dew was heavy on the grass, and the air had a smell that made me think of wood smoke and dry leaves.

He came out of the ship with me to say good-bye.

"Will you be back?" I asked him.

He buzzed wordlessly in a way I had begun to recognize; I think it was his version of a laugh. "I think not for a very long time. I have already neglected my work too much."

"This isn't your work—opening up new planets?"

"No. It is not so common a thing, that a race becomes ready for space travel. It has not happened anywhere in the galaxy for twenty thousand of your years. I believe, and I hope, that it will not happen again for twenty thousand more. No, I am ordinarily a maker of—you have not the word, it is like porcelain, but a different material. Perhaps some day you will see a piece that I have made. It is stamped with my name."

He held out his hand and I took it. It was an awkward grip; his hand felt unpleasantly dry and smooth to me, and I suppose mine was clammy to him. We both let go as soon as we decently could.

Without turning, he walked away from me up the ramp, I said, "Aza-Kra!"

"Yes?"

"Just one more question. The galaxy's a big place. What happens if you miss just one bloodthirsty race that's ready to boil out across the stars—or if nobody has the guts to go and do to them what you did to us?"

"Now you begin to understand," he said. "That is the question the people of Mars asked us about you twenty thousand years ago."

The story ends there, properly, but there's one more thing I want to say.

When Aza-Kra's ship lifted and disappeared, and I walked down to the bottom of the bluff and across the bridge into the city, I knew I was going back to a life that would be a lot different from the one I had known.

For one thing, the *Herald-Star* was all but done for when I came home: wrecked presses, half the staff gone, supplies running out. I worked hard for a little over a year trying to revive it out of sentiment, but I knew there were more important things to be done than publishing a newspaper.

Like everybody else, I got used to the changes in the world and in the people around me: to the peaceful, unworried feel of places that had been electric with tension; to the kids—the wonderful, incredible kids—to the new kind of excitement, the excitement that isn't like the night before execution, but like the night before Christmas.

But I hadn't realized how much I had changed myself, until something that happened a week ago.

I'd lost touch with Eli Freeman after the paper folded; I knew he had gone into pest control, but I didn't know where he was or what he was doing until he turned up one day on the wheat-and-dairy farm I help run, south of the Platte in what used to be Nebraska. He's the advance man for a fleet of spray planes working out of Omaha, aborting rabbits.

He stayed on for three days, lining up a few of the stiff-necked farmers in this area that don't believe in hormones or airplanes either; in his free time he helped with the harvest, and I saw a lot of him.

On his last night we talked late, working up from the old times to the new times and back again until there was nothing more to say. Finally, when we had both been quiet for a long time, he said something to me that is the only accolade I am likely to get, and oddly enough, the only one I want.

"You know, Bob, if it wasn't for that unique face of yours, it would be hard to believe you're the same guy I used to work for."

I said, "Hell, was I that bad?"

"Don't get shirty. You were okay. You didn't bleed the help or kick old ladies, but there just wasn't as much *to* you as there is now. I don't know," he said. "You're—more human."

More human.

Yes. We all are.

THE END